Strength in Petticoats

Dawn Hart

LEAF BY LEAF

Published by Leaf by Leaf
an imprint of Cinnamon Press,
Office 49019, PO Box 15113, Birmingham B2 2NJ
www.cinnamonpress.com

Print Edition ISBN 978-1-78864-874-5
British Library Cataloguing in Publication Data. A CIP record for this
book can be obtained from the British Library.

Designed and typeset in Adobe Caslon Pro by Cinnamon Press.
Cinnamon Press is represented by Inpress.

For Jack

Strength in Petticoats

Prologue

The two tiny coffins were lined up precisely on the altar in perfect symmetry. Side by side, their inhabitants passing from the world as they had arrived into it.

Made from grainy oak, sourced from the neighbouring forests, they perched silently in resplendent glory. The corner joints lovingly carved by the gnarled hands of local craftsmen; the brass handles glinted in the light of adjacent candles as they, in turn, dripped waxen tears onto the marble floor. These molten globules slid from burning to frozen as the congregation watched the hypnotic cascade.

Most striking to the sensibilities of mourners was the width of these vessels—almost equal in breadth as in length. But they commented in hushed, reverent tones; there was a need to contain the wide shoulders, strong arms, and muscular legs of each twin. Reflections of their solid, energy infused bodies filtered through curtains of memories.

Inside the coffins the two compact bodies lay, tucked in identical satin nests, deep purple to evoke the Passion. Carefully placed atop, the wrestlers' masks sat proudly at the head of each like talismans—one the colour of a drop of scarlet blood, the other a drop of deep turquoise ocean. The gaudiness of the primary-coloured satin caught shafts of kaleidoscopic light channelled through stained glass, shouting its presence amidst the muted, organic hues of the chapel's ancient stone walls and pews worn thin by worship and prayer.

Mourners solemnly filed past the coffins. The chapel was a cacophony of every sense and sound; the heady smell of religious incense and lilies permeated; the catholic wafer and wine tasted bitter on each mourner's tongue as internally they tried to reconcile having been betrayed by their Lord—how could one so merciful allow the twins to be taken in such an undignified, callous way?

At the back of the church a trio of policemen , conspicuous behind sunglasses despite the dark cavernous chapel. The agitation of one was palpable as he shifted his weight from foot to foot—his attempts to steady himself by staring at his morning-polished shoes were fruitless. Keeping a subtle presence, the policemen had each come to pay their respects as local citizens, while professionally hawk eyed, watching the congregation's every move for a sign of accidental self-betrayal—a delighted glint placing themselves in the upper hierarchy of mourners, way beyond their social standing.

The shuffle of summer shoes could be heard as each mourner passed the altar, showing respect and making the sign of the cross, forehead, chest, left shoulder, right shoulder... over and over. Women bowed heads and lowered eyes beneath black lace veils inhaling the acrid aroma of naphthalene, while their gnarled hands gripped cotton embroidered handkerchiefs. The men of the town squeaked in their stiff leather shoes and starched linen suits, which clung to their backs in the torpid heat.

The twins' mother stood alone; her jet-black dress

draped from her shrunken shoulders like weeds clinging to rocks long after the tide had retreated. Her body could hold no more weight. Her eyes were bowed in reverence to the Madonna, but also to avoid multiple gazes, which wanted to look into hers to vicariously understand grief, and to avoid them for fear that her pain might be contagious. Occasionally, she glanced over her left shoulder to the shadow cast by the heavy oak door, hoping the twins' father would emerge, step forward and briefly stand shoulder to shoulder with her again. Yet would she recognise him now, after the passing of so many years, so much life?

A solitary figure sat at the aisle end of the final back pew. Ramrod, the vertebrae of her spine precisely stacked each atop the other, she looked directly ahead. As a stranger within this closed community, she drew attention, aroused suspicion. Her flamboyant dress did little to lower raised eyebrows. Her skirt was tiered and comprised of concertina-pleated blue taffeta. Around her shoulders was draped a mustard filigree crocheted shawl. Her hair, glossy, black as a crow; below a pencil-straight parting, her carefully plaited style divided into two heavy ropes, falling parallel to her spine. On her lap she held a small black bowler hat, like a sleeping, curled cat.

Outside the chapel, it was a crisp day—one that held ironic optimism. The birds carelessly sang, forgetting to pay due respect. Blossom blew from the almond trees, imitating the confetti of weddings, which Emilio and Emiliano would never enjoy; they would forever be frozen as young men on the precipice of fame and success.

A gaggle of local journalists gathered at the chapel gates in a jostle, caught between the desire to honour the passing and the ambition to capture the story and claim their media fame with the photo of the most distraught, confused mourner. Privately, each person in this emotionally charged scene wondered quietly: *Does the murderer walk amongst us?*

One

The twins were born into the good catholic Belasco family of the Sierra Madre de Oaxaca Mountains, just as the century was drawing to its close. The ancient landscape permeated the psyche of the locals, the pine forests stretching to stroke the sky, the moisture trapped in the air, the majesty of the mountains. They moved about their daily business with timeless grace, instinctively knowing their lives were fleeting shudders of a moth's wings.

Maria developed a habit of rubbing her hand gently over her belly as it swelled early in her pregnancy. She counted her blessings from God not once but twice. "Stay safe little ones," she would utter quietly to herself, *for you are the small, precious answers to my prayers.* "After so many months, turning into so many years, God has finally brought you to me." This new life force: God had heard the prayers whispered from her soul on bended knee night after night. *Please let me be a mother—to give all this love I'm carrying to a child who I promise I will protect and nurture for all eternity. This is all I will ever ask you for, just grant me this one thing.*

She kneels to pray each morning, the floorboards worn thin by generations of the devout, the only sound outside her window the braying of the restless donkey. Her spoken voice offers thanks, gratitude: her quieter, more secret voice is infused with the ambivalence of doubt suffused with hope. *I know I must keep my side of the bargain. I know I must be grateful and not wish for more than I am allowed. But if there is one more thing to be given, please let these embryos be boy children. For then my marriage will also be saved. Please allow me this one more mercy. Let my husband walk tall in this place, in his place—the proud father of two magnificent boys.*

"Chicharito, chicharito," she sang, clutching the magical celluloid presented to her by the doctor, a warm face in the cold clinical hospital room. The two soft edged shapes of her kumquat sized soon to be sons holding each other in a tight embrace homed inside the protection of her womb. Heartbeat after heartbeat pumping blood bound into her body. The two little beans with their smooth rounded edges blended into one being, so tight was their embrace. She whispered murmurings of love to them. She chanted thanks to their creator, a secret pact of thoughts she should share with no other for fear that to question her blessing may make it fail and be withdrawn.

Her belly grows and grows. She relishes the sensation of her skin stretching, the animalistic invasion of angry red lines like the claw marks of a scared creature break out in a jagged pattern. The babies leave her breathless, even before her third trimester is in sight, squishing her diaphragm into a convex arch above which her breath has little space to dance. The days are hotter and stickier, or so they seem; a burning creeps up the back of her neck hourly without warning. Eventually and reluctantly, she must allow her obstinate cousin, Margarita, to assume command of her market stall as she is no longer able to stand in the heat of the day, bargaining and swatting flies from her oranges, tomatoes and ombre dahlias.

As the weeks passed, Maria became increasingly unable to dispel an ethereal sense of something about the future being a threat to her familiar life. She would awake in the night and before her eyes could focus on the darkness, ominous shapes lingering in the corners of the room overwhelmed her and forced her to close her eyes again, retreat into her body. To confide in Juan Carlos as he slept deeply beside her was not an option, as honourable as he was; she knew he was a man given to occupying a world of certainty. Even before their marriage vows had knitted their lives as one, he had often displayed a streak of impatience towards her when she described her wilder imaginative world.

Her twentieth week of pregnancy arrived. Taking the bus in the midday heat for another ultrasound, Juan Carlos had to shake the lingering embarrassment of the taunting by his work colleagues that he should forsake a day's wages to make this journey into what was perceived as a woman's world. On his lap he cradled the wicker basket with their lunch of almonds, bread, and chicken, so they would not have to pay city prices in a café. He teased her as she tucked her knitting into the basket—another tiny white cardigan was about to be cast off. He was unable to resent the cost of the wool for she was clearly knitting her anxiety away, but nonetheless he tenderly teased her that their twins would have a whole wardrobe of tiny clothes but would have to run naked by their first birthdays.

Sitting firmly in this alien city that circumstance had accidentally propelled her into, Maria knew she did not belong at the hospital. White-coated doctors in horn-rimmed spectacles, precise neat nurses in practical shoes and tied back hair, marched along corridors, purposeful, nodding greetings at colleagues in a silent dance of which Maria had no knowledge. Nature was kept at bay by large, sealed windows behind which landscaped gardens could be observed but not touched or smelt. The heavy stench of disinfection forced her into a hormonal retch. She hated those medical terms, which bounced off the walls in staccato consonants, and longed to be alone and talk of poetry and love and song to her twins. Her daily life was lived so close to nature and the turnings of the sun and the moon, she could find no route to weave it together in this hostile building. But the sepia image of her babies in the previous scan had been so wonderful she longed to witness their awe-inspiring growth from the size of almonds to that of tangerines.

The nurse's soft-featured face became tight, the muscles around her eyes twitching as she ran the sensor over Maria's sticky belly while examining the screen.

'Can you be sure about your dates?' she asked. 'Is there a chance that you could be less than 20 weeks, say about 12 weeks?'

Maria was sure; her body always had regularity to it, in tune with the lunar cycles and the rising and ebbing tides. Every month she knew the precise day, even the hour when her body would bleed. The youthful doctor, with bright eyes and a smooth chin, was ushered into the already claustrophobically small room, and peered closely at the screen, tilting his head one side to another.

Once she had dressed, she and Juan Carlos were taken to an even smaller room with uneven legged plastic chairs and a whirring overhead fan. Her mind was determined to protect her body and its precious cargo, and she focused her attention on the basket Juan Carlos held firmly on his lap, clutching it to his chest with both of his muscular arms. Although she tried to block the gently spoken doctor's words, some still slipped through her filter like tobacco grains through a cheap cigarette; 'unusually small; well-developed; family history.'

Dazed, she went home, confused how on the inward bus journey everything had felt full of hope and joy and now there were adjustments. Was this a blessing or a curse? The future story she had created in her imagination for her babies had to be rewritten, but her mind couldn't draw a new picture. Not yet. Had she caused this by knitting so many tiny garments? Had this made her babies determined to remain tiny versions of themselves? The urban landscape morphed into farmland and untamed hills, slipping past like a movie she watched as Juan Carlos sat silently by her side. His presence was no longer the solid, strong figure she had known; it was cumbersome—one more thing to contend with. Did the celluloid she had tucked into the basket below the uneaten husks of bread show her babies floating amniotically, yet clinging so tightly each to the other, because this was how they would have to survive in a world in which the conventional was prince and king? There was nothing familiar to anchor herself. She floated high and hovered like a dragonfly looking down, observing herself, wondering who she now was.

*

Fourteen weeks and two days creaked by, hours passing to days, days to weeks and finally the weeks drew into months. Maria and Juan Carlos withdrew further and further into their internal worlds—hers of a growing love for her babes and his into increasing disorientation and fear. Spring followed winter with an assuredness of rebirth until on a day which had seemed as unremarkable as any other, the evening sun set, and the universe's puppet master drew up the perfect toenail of a waxing crescent moon. Twinges coursed through Maria's body heralding a labour set to be more challenging than any housework or market stall toil she had known. Initial excitement engulfed her, twinges of anticipation, before the reality of the pain took hold: this was seven whole days and nights beyond her due date, the swelling of her oedemic ankles was unbearable, the space in her lungs for her breath only allowing sips of air to enter her body. Coupled with the anxiety of the pending revelation of the secret, that which she and Juan Carlos had held so close for an age now, she just wanted to give birth to these two tiny, perfectly formed people. Juan Carlos had reassured her the villagers were their friends and had been so for generation upon generation—they would not pass judgement, nor see the twins as a visiting curse. If only she could share his surety. If only she had the same fearless confidence they would not be ostracised from all that was ever certain.

Maria flung open the wooden shutters and let the late shafts of sunlight penetrate her bedroom with splendour, bouncing off the turquoise peeling paint of her ancient chest of drawers. The scent of her carefully tended bougainvillaea slid in and ingratiated itself into her nostrils. The storm curtains would need to be closed tight before dusk crept in to keep both the night and its creatures at bay, but for now it was glorious to feel the unfettered air on the nape of her neck as she drew her cascading thick hair into a tightly bound ponytail.

"We should get you into the car and to the hospital," whispered Juan Carlos, as he stroked her clammy forehead.

"Come, I've filled the tank with petrol. Your bag is here. You can lean on one arm here." He gestured a mixture of an embrace and a crutch. "I'll carry your bag in my other hand. It's all going to be fine."

She pushed his hand away and groaned. She wanted to keep this moment timeless. The sanctity of her pregnancy was hers alone to hold, or to break. But the contractions gripped her belly like an iron fist, invading her body to its core and telling her that sense should prevail. As the chorus of cicadas in the garden grew bolder, she knew it was time for the twins to be released from their amniotic sanctuary and into the humid, oppressive night.

Juan Carlos drove with an erratic blend of acute caution and heedless speed to transport them all to the delivery room. After a seemingly unending journey down from the mountain village in the rusted but methodically maintained car, they turned the corner. Rising from the road, swirling with dusk dust, they saw the clinically white, sterile cathedralesque hospital preening itself as a symbol of progress.

Maria braced herself to travel into this unknown territory.

As the town hall clock confidently struck eleven, Emilio seized centre stage from his not yet born twin and arrived dramatically with a gush of fluid and blood. Veronica, Maria's midwife, for once showed lines of tenderness around the contours of her pursed lips. Maria's fear of her led to her obedience; village stories of midwifery had led her to expect a joyful companion to nurture and encourage her with smiles and ancient songs passed down from ancestral women. Conversely, Veronica was of her own mould-weathered skin with enough facial hair to form a full beard, and a shelf-shaped bosom protruding from her chest, straining at the buttons of her pale green, over-washed clinical outfit. As Emilio shot into the world like a cannonball, Veronica wiped the buttery vernix from his eyes, unceremoniously plonked him on Maria's sweat-soaked left breast, and issued the instruction she should push his twin out before she had time to catch her breath.

Maria inhaled the sweet *queso fresco* of her firstborn before she bore down into the most exquisite pain known to womankind and within minutes felt the crowning of her second son, ready to make up the pair as their umbilical separation began.

The double birth, in rapid succession, shocked Maria's body into an endless tremble that would never quite leave her. Years later, when they made their own co-dependent way in the world, whenever she saw her boys from a distance, her stomach, and strong legs shook a little as if the memory of their birth was still lodged forever in her organs and soft tissues. But for now she basked in the sense of the universe standing still as it allowed the stars to realign above them. At that moment, unaware this would be the last time she would ever experience being completely happy and at peace.

After an efficient wash, the twins' separate identities were written onto their bracelets:

Baby Sanchez 1: 2.1kgs

Baby Sanchez 2: 2.05 kgs

A confirmatory look passed between the now-parents—the names they had played with on the long uncomfortable pregnant nights fitted these boys. Their mother and their father both knew that Baby Sanchez 1 was their Emilio and Baby Sanchez 2 was Emiliano. They already had identities.

To Maria's eyes, they were beautifully formed, albeit tinier versions of most other babies delivered that night. However, the mutterings and calling up of antenatal notes by the hospital team confirmed that her secret was now visible for the world to pass judgement on. To others, a glimpse of two hydrocephalic foreheads was heralding alarm bells that this bastion of clinical perfection had been penetrated by not one, but two babies deviating from the standard scale. Maria asked for the air conditioning to be turned up to quench the fire in her belly rising to her chest; the tigress in her was unfurling, knowing she had to rapidly learn how to protect these little vessels in need of her love.

When Emiliano was placed into Juan Carlos's arms, she heard him whisper into his son's tiny ear. She couldn't hear the words, but his face held a tender promise, and the baby wriggled his body closer to his father's chest.

'He is perfect, my love,' Juan Carlos said as he held his second born to his chest, 'just perfect. My beautiful boy.'

Maria adjusted on the bed, tucked the first twin into the crook of her arm as if she'd always been a mother, and asked, 'Can I see him?'

The hospital clock ticked clinically; the second hand exerting a supreme effort to push itself forward. A lump rose in her throat, her palms moist. 'Can I see him? Just for one minute?'

Juan Carlos looked up at her with an unfamiliar tear in the corner of his eye. 'What a beautiful, beautiful child.' With this parting comment, he placed the second twin into her spare open arm and left the room, his rubber-soled boots creating squeaks on the sterile floor to accompany his heavy-footed paces.

Now unable to wipe the sweat from her forehead as both arms and hands were full to overflowing with her babes, Maria looked down at her second twin. For the first time since arriving at the hospital the three of them were alone, as they had been for the last eight and a half months, but now she could see them, smell them, touch them. Which twin would she love most? Could she love them both equally?

She kissed the forehead of her second born and turned her sense of wonderment to her first son. Whispering love into each of his ears, landing butterfly kisses on each eyelid, gliding her vision down his pink downy-haired arms, noting the chubbiness of his tiny hands, and then counting his digits, one, two, three, four, five, six, seven, eight, nine… an unknown sensation prickled the back of her neck. A migraine was arriving, an unwelcome visitor, induced by the unrelenting fluorescent tube light. Screwing her eyes she counted once more: one, two, three, four, five, six, seven, eight, nine. His thumb, where was his right thumb? How could he only have nine digits? There were without a doubt eight tiny, tiny fingers, and on his left hand a reassuringly firm thumb. But even in her elegiac, floating post-birth state of mind, it was impossible for her to deny that on his right hand was an absence and in its place a smooth foreboding nub of bone.

Two

Consuelo insisted her daughter accompany her to work, but Lillibet, watching other children being led, tiny hands inside larger ones, in cotton dresses pressed with love, carrying small knapsacks on their backs, longed to be dropped at the brightly painted kindergarten gates. Beyond the gates was a tantalising freedom. Instead, she was obliged to spend her days practising invisibility. While Maria brought new lives into this world, Consuelo, on the other side of the equator, scrubbed and cleaned, ironed, and dusted, swept and washed. Making no sound, creating no mischief, in this beautiful house Lillibet learned to be there but not; in her tender young heart she already sensed those who lived here, in the beautiful house, the people for whom her mother worked, were not themselves, beautiful.

The house was full of lavish objects, a magpie's treasure trove: trinkets glinted on the window ledges, plush cushions had peacock patterns embossed on them and the immaculately polished cutlery matched in neat sets like an ideal family, arranged in the compartments of a green baize-lined walnut box. Wind never entered via the windows, rather an occasional gentle breeze suggestive of the flutter of fairy wings. The walled garden created a haven from the dusty streets and kept the hawkers beyond the tall, locked gate. Striped gourds grew across the ground in organised rows, strawberries poked from terracotta domes and passion flowers cast spirals between the branches of bottle green trellis. Nothing was left to the randomness of Nature herself. Yet the people of the house, rather than counting their blessings, perpetually complained and criticised Lillibet's mother in cruel tongues. They were passively unkind to Lillibet, not addressing her in any tongue, speaking above her head, negating her presence. Lillibet felt if she and her family lived in this house, they would be happy and generous of spirit to the humble people who cleaned up after their every step.

Lillibet and Consuelo lived in a small town at the foot of the Uturuncu Volcano. Although dormant for decades, the volcano's potential for eruption ran through the lifeblood of the locals, making them volatile. The air, ash free for generations, was clean and fresh. Acerola, cashews, and nectarines grew in abundance and Consuelo cultivated corn and soya beans in their small, sun-trapped garden. It was only later, looking back through a lens polished with experience, that Lillibet saw her family as humbly industrious by nature and necessity. Her adult self observed, like an anthropologist, how they had been allocated roles that followed function like a machine, keeping it all running day after day. Lillibet as the eldest child, obliged to trudge daily in her mother's weary footsteps. Valeria, her younger sister, remained meanwhile with their grandmother Beatriz, enjoying the pleasures of play under the supervision of the kindly woman, while her father Garron worked at the sulphur mine, and Consuelo trudged to the beautiful house.

In the evenings when all returned home as a family, Lillibet was allowed to play in the street with the other local children until dusk crept in. There was an equity in their worn, scrubbed clothes, ill-fitting shoes passed down from older siblings, and frayed skipping ropes. She would run in and out of her aunt's kitchen, relishing the sensation of her cheek being stroked while being gently chided for her unruly behaviour by his woman who was always chopping vegetables, stirring pots, or mixing spices.

Sunday was Consuelo's day of rest when the people from the big house had to take responsibility for their own wellbeing. She would dress Lillibet in a pristine white dress, brush the tangles from her hair and tie it with an emerald satin ribbon. The child then would sit waiting, tapping her patent black shoes while her mother got herself ready. Lillibet was not allowed out to play in the dusty street for fear she might sully her Sunday best clothes. Each Sunday the same: after an eternity, her mother emerged from the parental bedroom in her pollera-her skirt, so broad it created the impression her hips had doubled in size. Falling to cover her calves, protecting her decency by hiding what had long been considered the woman's most erotic body part. The kingfisher blue taffeta had layers like the terraces of a coffee farm; the net petticoat, the enagua, crackled like bonfires as her mother walked in her foot-shod flat pumps. A mustard shawl was wrapped around the broadest part of her shoulders, crossed at her waist, and held at her breast with an antique tarnished brass brooch in the shape of a kantuta flower. Her long dark hair was parted with pencil-sharp accuracy and scraped back into two heavy plaits. The whole outfit completed by her black felt bowler hat, perched precariously. atop her head to denote a married woman. How Lillibet longed for a time when she too would be allowed to dress like this—to look this majestic, to have womanly hips swaying metronomically. First though she must be schooled in the cholita values so she no longer knew her true nature from what had been instilled into her bones: she must learn never to lie, never to steal and the honour in work.

If only others realised how beautiful her mother looked. Leaving the house hand in hand, they walked their route to church along the winding, cobbled street, snaking up towards the bells calling the faithful to prayer. The local shops closed in observance of the Sabbath, but that did not quell the noises of the street; men sat at aged wooden tables in the shade of trees outside the café, slamming down backgammon pieces and debating politics while gesticulating wildly. Women swept their cottage paths and the pavements beyond, gossiping about any absent neighbour. A couple of dogs lay in the dust, lethargically swatting flies from their rumps with their tails. The church stood in solitary splendour at the pinnacle of the hill, visible for miles; although recently whitewashed, it was still tarnished with a covering of lingering beige volcano dust.

Lillibet, holding tight so the tendons in her forearm ached, found comfort in the calloused palms of Consuelo's broad, sun-cracked hands. *Squeeze me tighter mum, and tighter still, rapid so I know you love me. And if there is a god, make this Sunday different.* But as they proceeded through the neighbourhood, her hopes were dashed; her mother walked with her eyes set unblinking straight ahead while local men eyed her with irritation. Beyond the crackling of her mother's skirt, three hissed syllables were all Lillibet's ears could tune into as they spat: 'Cholita. Cholita. Cholita,' an echo following them like a venomous snake. What was the meaning of these words? Copying her mother's unflinching stare, she wondered why the words carried such spite? A hurt she felt somewhere deep. *Stay proud, stay erect, mirror mum. These men will not be allowed to inflict shame on neither me nor her*—this woman, she knew, was beautiful, and under her nurturing guidance she could one day be as proud, as beautiful.

*

Lillibet longed to unfurl. She was devoted to Consuelo, the throb of her love pressing against her heart chambers, yet as she embarked on her teenage years, she knew she wanted more from her life than her mother's lowly ambitions for her; she knew she wanted the same educational opportunities as the boys she had grown up with; she knew she did not want her future pre-ordained, constrained by the assumption of marriage to a local boy, children soon to follow the wedding at a respectable interval and the consequent grandchildren. She did not want to play it safe—her spirit craved adventure, but adventure that did not betray her cholita roots. She would always be a cholita and wear this as proudly as the generations before her. She would be like a fern that unfurls its fronds with grace and elegance before the garden has realised its sheer beauty. And then there would be no going back, not for herself, nor for those around her. She would drop a stone into a pond and relish the inevitability of ripple after ripple, expanding energy begetting energy.

Typical of other cholitas, Consuelo wore her heritage with defiant pride, through her clothing and spirit. Time past was very much present in her time present. Way, way back, before the cholitas had become tourist attractions, curiosities, they had sat among the wider population as symbols of shame, as deep as an undiscovered well. There they went, the embodiment of an intermingling of bodily fluids between an indigenous person and a colonial invader. Maybe a moment of force, maybe of forbidden passion. And resulting from this intermingling of sweat and semen a blended blood, which refused to hide her face. "Cholla, cholla, cholla,' came the cry.

The Spanish invaders had embarked on a project, so common among colonials—the building of a railroad. An order of bowler hats, typical of the style of western gentlemen, was placed to keep the beating sun rays off the labourers' exposed skulls. Blame was projected in all directions when the shipment arrived; no one knew how, where, or why it had gone awry, but these hats were miniature, far too small to be fit for purpose, far too large to be comedic. Variations of the next part of the tale snake in as many directions as every good story passed through generations, yet somehow the tiny hats ended up on the proud heads of the cholitas, and there they remained.

*

Consuelo had been brought up as a rural woman who worked the land and became buried in the grinding domesticity of an economically poor household. Yet as in any land in which the siren of capitalist 'progress' is heard, the generation born after her gravitated towards the throbbing pulse of the towns, in search of more. The young cholitas wanted more adventure, more bling, and bigger horizons. It would be the generation after Lillibet who realised that less is more, and this grasping would be replaced with the stories of the old days. But for now, Lillibet is our focus. It is she we will follow as she explores the areas of this town where her mother would never go for fear of disapproval; it will be she, along with her friends, who will carve out a new place for the cholitas as they unflinchingly meet the critical eyes cast upon them.

Lillibet and her friends did not sit around in semi-darkened rooms plotting to overthrow the system; neither were they supported by wealthy benefactors who acted as puppeteers, engineering others to make the change they wanted to see. Rather, they were just a group of teenage girls who simultaneously realised they wanted more, and that there was a power in not standing alone. They stood on the shoulders of giants, the strong women of history who had shown what was possible when women act on courage and stand firm in the public sphere. They also stood on the shoulders of those quieter women who chipped at edifices built of rock and stone to bring about change so, so gradually, methodically.

Their crinkling petticoats, bowler hats, glinting gold jewellery ensured their presence was always noticeable—in that respect they did not need to herald themselves. They wanted to be visible in the prohibited bus seats, at the political meetings, in the gyms and shops. And they were. But a curious thing happened—they went beyond acceptance, and unexpectedly became fashionable!

Last year a well-known New York photographer, Sam Moore, had accepted his editor's commission to "capture those girls for a spread before anyone else does". He seized the opportunity, greedily—the cholitas had occupied a space in his already well populated imagination since last year. The micro financing charity he donated to every quarter had suggested he contribute to a loan to "Candy: looking to expand her textile enterprise". Candy, in her photograph, had a defiance, or was it pride; enough to make him wonder about her daily life, family, loves and dreams. She was somehow more real, more three dimensional than the other people being paraded in portrait photos for westerners to support in their entrepreneurial endeavours. Sam had paid the full sum loan that Candy was requesting, a total of 2% of his salary that month. A wash of pride had engulfed him for the week he played with the idea that maybe one day he could meet Candy and how she would embrace him with the gratitude she felt at his lifting her out of poverty. He was sure he could melt that hard, proud look into a joyous smile. Of course he was going to accept the commission to spend a day in a hot dusty town, snapping reels of choilitas on catwalks and if not bumping into Candy herself, maybe an encounter with another of these glorious creatures was on the cards!

Sam researched the cholitas during his south bound flight—their history, dress, values. By the time he landed on foreign soil he felt he knew all there was to know about them. He was ready to use the power of his camera to give them access to the glitterati of New York, with the bonus of the kudos it might just bring him. On checking into his hotel room he rummaged in his case in the hope of having packed an outfit more suitable to this sticky humidity. The best he could manage was to swap his black turtle neck for a tight-fitting black t shirt—why hadn't he put in his trainers instead of another pair of boots? Maybe he could buy a lighter shirt, something more vivid. On stepping out onto the pavement, leaving the hotel's protective air conditioning, he tugged at the front of his t shirt as it clung to his belly, made slightly rounded by his New York winter indulgence in pizza and bagels. It was time to get back into shape, hit the gym on his return, maybe change up his wardrobe. For now he needed to focus on his commission—the editor had been specific about his brief—set aside for him was a double spread in which he would portray, in glorious technicolor, the young cholitas dancing, talking, and going about their daily business, to bring them to life. After all they were the latest thing! Now, where to find them? Sam stepped to the edge of the kerb to hail a cab, but faltered as he realised, he wasn't sure which direction he would ask the driver to head. The weight of his camera bag dug into his shoulder and his phone wasn't picking up wifi. Maybe this wasn't going to be so straightforward.

*

Fashion is at its peacock height on the catwalk, and this was the place Lillibet found herself at a cool city club on a stifling Friday afternoon. The club had been commandeered by the fashion house and decked to resemble a mountain village with which Lillibet was oh so familiar from long Sunday afternoon visits to aunts, godmothers, and great uncles. Yet the chic city dwellers had probably never set foot in those places, never smelt the almond trees in blossom, or tasted the air as clear as a forest stream. On this afternoon, the poverty and the beauty of village life had been airbrushed out and sanitised, forming a backdrop to the cholita fashion show. There were no dragonflies flitting amongst the guests, and the food served on silver platters bore little resemblance to the tostadas and black beans cooked by her grand aunts.

Guests gathered on orderly rows of dressed chairs to see and be seen. Lillibet was the first model to flounce onto the catwalk, sashaying her hips as she'd been instructed, making her pollera enlarge her bodily movements. Everything was amplified; her cheeks blushed with rounded cartoon dollops of rouge, her jewellery tinkled as she walked, and her petticoat was a bright emerald green, contrasting with the scarlet taffeta of her skirt.

Sam arrived in time to witness this spectacle. Within seconds he felt he was straddling worlds, precariously so. His mission wasn't unique—this town was now host to a trickle-like invasion of thin young adults head to toe in understated yet overpriced black, pointing long lenses wherever they pleased. Cholitas studied in their natural habitat.

The crowd, packed in tightly on gold and red seats, called out in 'oooohs' and 'aaaahs' as the models flounced, as if they had never turned their back on a cholita in a city street. Sam, for the first time in his career, experienced a prickling embarrassment as he hid behind his camera lens. He would fulfil his commission as always, capture these women without letting his readers' know of the inauthenticity he had become party to. A power shift had happened in plain sight, and he wasn't sure if he liked it.

Lillibet permitted herself a quiet smile as she left the

catwalk, her parade having been successfully executed. She knew her audience had been captured between awe and guilt; but she also knew this was just the beginning, the place from which she would begin to take up more space in the world, breath more oxygen into her lungs.

*

The emotion was too swollen, too expansive to be contained within the constraints of the small, box shaped waiting room. Overhead the ceiling fan whirred precariously, filling an overbearing silence. The storm shutters banged with metronomic rhythm as a wind danced its way in from the sea; the storm would surely arrive before the night was out.

Maria, shifting her post-pregnant weight from one buttock to another against the peeling paint of the institutional chair, riveted her eyes on her twins as her decoy. *If I keep my gaze focused, I can avoid eye contact with the other post-partum mothers. Is this jealousy or envy I feel towards them? They're judging me. I know they're looking at me with pity, at my boys with disgust.*

The talk at the christening echoed endlessly in her soul. The tones hushed, fragments of judgements which no amount of marzipan biscuits and sugared almonds could sweeten. The carefully wrapped gifts, given in pairs for each twin as gestures of fairness, sat on the table suggesting generosity. She imagined moving around the room greeting, smiling, offering tea and sometimes 'something stronger.' Guests drifting out on the terrace, basking in the late morning sun, whispers trailing with them. 'Why has she done this?' 'What made her invite the devil into her belly?' 'If we mix with her and those two small babies, will we also be cursed?' 'Never has any such thing happened in the village before.' 'What did the priest say?'

Stroking each twin on their left cheek, her heart beat faster as they both turned their heads in search of her swollen, gorged breasts. Each baby was overly warm but snug in their love-knitted tiny woollen cardigans. She absentmindedly rubbed the nub of Emilio's thumb joint, a preoccupation becoming habitual, as if by kneading love into it she would enable him to grow a thumb to mirror his brother's. Emiliano was already self-soothing with ferocious sucking motions on his right thumb, as if sucking for himself and his brother. *My second-born is going to need so much more of my love and strength than his brother. That one is already showing the very first signs of independence—he will be just fine making his way in the world. But my smallest jewel…*

The shifting of the sun's angle into the late morning brightness reminded her that her appointment time had long passed. *Everyone is being called in before me. I'm not imagining it. That one, the woman with the rounded cheeks and sweet baby girlishness, arrived after me I'm sure. Maybe her appointment was earlier. Maybe not. Four women have gone in ahead, my mind isn't too addled to notice. My babies are being leapfrogged over, the other, perfectly formed babes ushered through, cooed over, weighed, tapped, and cuddled while my Emilio and Emiliano are neglected.* Outside the window she focused on a stray mongrel scavenging scraps of food amongst discarded vegetable peelings, while the old man sat outside the café, eking out one cup of coffee for the whole morning, threw a stone at the dog as it cowered with learned helplessness.

Juan Carlos stood with his back to the clinical room, his gaze resting through the dust-covered sealed window on the distant mountains and the village he had only recently left. His fingers rubbed the wooden rosary in his pocket. *I should free him*, thought Maria, *liberate him from the gossip's daily speculations, those who have made it their business to talk endlessly on how his manhood has produced not one, but two tiny sons. Those who relish the misfortune of others. Tell him—I should tell him to go far to a place where he is unknown, to start life afresh. Life lived under this barrage of judgement will be tough for me and the twins, but surely this is better than the screaming silence, which is now the mood music of our marriage.* Her babies now fully occupied her heart; every muscle and sinew stretched to accommodate her all-consuming love—there seemed to be no space for any love for anyone else, not even her husband.

Juan Carlos had never been an articulate man. His language was of the soil, the sky, and the weather. The land was a more reliable companion than any human. As one of eleven siblings, his background was based on practicalities rather than emotions, and so their farm had functioned as one giant organism with many tentacles. Juan Carlos, along with his youngest brother, was responsible for shepherding the sheep in their daily grassy forage. The brothers wandered hills barefooted, carrying hooked wooden staffs from early light until the setting of the sun, learning to be alone with their thoughts. It had never occurred to him that life could be other than as predictable and reliable as the turning seasons, that anything could interrupt the flow of the natural world.

Maria and Juan Carlos had met at the spring cattle

market in Izameal. On that day, as the canary yellow buildings glinted against a turquoise sky. He was neither buying nor selling but came with his brothers to enjoy a brief interlude from the day to day. They each donned their Sunday best: corduroy trousers held with fraying braces, worn over crisply ironed white cotton shirts. They felt smart, dapper, knowing as a group they drew the eyes of envy for their youthful athleticism. Although feigning disinterest, each brother hoped to survey the girls from neighbouring villages. As young men in their prime, the turning generations dictated it would soon be their time to each catch, court and cajole a local girl.

Juan Carlos spotted Maria across the cattle ring; she looked familiar and unknown. He recognised her as the youngest daughter of the Lopez family, known for their abundant fruit harvests. Yet somehow, she was different from the same girl he'd seen the previous autumn: although still trim, her body was more rounded, contoured. Her deep black hair was piled high, tendrils escaping and adhering to the droplets of sweat on her slender neck. She was selling oranges and hardboiled eggs from bright baskets she swung from each arm. Smiling broadly at customers, she exchanged wares for coins, slipping them deftly into the deep front pocket of her cotton apron. This smile was contagious, and her customers willingly echoed it, the transaction taking on an air of spring frivolity.

Juan Carlos stroked the few coins inside his trouser pocket, knowing they were his toll price to gain a smile and a ripe, puckered nectarine. He muttered his rehearsed lines over and over, but even whispering them to himself, knowing their stiltedness, cast a blush across his ruddy cheeks.

'What a grand day for us to be out in the sunshine.'

'How is it possible for you to look so cool and composed in this blazing heat?' Or a little more daring: 'These fruits are the ripest I've seen, I'm sure they taste delicious.'

Taking care to appear unhurried, he walked to her, hand in pocket, thumb worrying the cuticles of his ring finger, placing each foot with unfamiliar caution. Breathing slowly, composed, Maria cast her hazel eyes up to meet his. He faltered. 'Two nectarines please.'

By the following spring their wedding had been arranged by her sisters. Although it was to be a simple affair as neither family had wealth to spare, love and goodwill were abundant, and they were sent on their married life to midday church bells ringing, the tinkling of laughter, orange blossom and the rustle of silk, the taste of honey-soaked pastries and the braying laughter of young men. Two golden rings, heirlooms from other now long-deceased brides and grooms, bound them in holy matrimony.

*

The oppressive air inside the sealed windows of the hospital contrasted sharply with the freshness of the mountain air he was so used to. Juan Carlos longed to be outside where he could breathe more easily. His shoulders were heavy, trapped within the well-worn shirt previously so comforting now prickling, irritating the skin on his neck where earlier he had meticulously shaved. Pulling at the offending collar like an adolescent at a wedding, he felt Maria's gaze penetrating the back of his neck, willing him to turn. But she would see through his eyes: how he was unable to forgive her. And then there would be no going back. Why had she allowed the devil into her body and produced these Little People? He so wanted to love his sons, so why such strong shame? Oh to not care what others thought or said, whether with their voices or excruciating looks of pity. If only he could be sure his personality was strong enough to stand alone, against the crowd. Or at least shoulder to shoulder with Maria.

The heat in this room was unbearable. He was not meant for a world of waiting rooms, leaflets, and tests, which his sons would fail, always fail.

'I will wait in the car,' he said, as he left the room without meeting his wife's eyes or looking at his babies.

Poised and still, Maria stared straight ahead, into her uncertain future.

Three

Maria finished sweeping the kitchen floor, propped her broom behind the door, wiped her chapped hands, and with a twinge in her lower back, picked up her mother's old straw basket ready to go to the market, the start of another long day trying to earn a living to support her small family of three.

She stroked the hair out of Emilio's eyes as his thick, curly fringe flopped forward. Still stroking, she said to Emiliano: 'Keep an eye on the clock and remember when the big hand reaches the red spot, it's time for you both to go to school. Make sure you wear your sun hats, it's scorching today. Your lunches are packed here, and your schoolbooks are already in your bags. And make sure your brother eats plenty of breakfast, he's getting too thin.'

Kissing each in turn on their foreheads, the daily wrench in the pit of her stomach knotted, an unease that she might lose control of her bowels. Despite the daily repetition of this well-rehearsed scenario, these somatic manifestations of her troubled mind never abated. Swallowing the lump in her throat and avoiding the gaze of four beseeching eyes, she hurried out of the paint peeling front door.

Emilio chased the small tomatoes and lumps of cheese around his breakfast plate with a fork, occasionally lifting it to his expectant mouth. The time of day before his mum departed the house was precious; he was calm and protected by her domestic presence. There was a comfort in the regularity of her routine; the wiping down of faded kitchen surfaces, the way she took warmed bread out of the oven and placed it on the worn walnut bread board, how she polished the taps until they caught the dance of morning sun rays on bright metal. The kitchen was his favourite room. Everything was mismatched and familiar. His finger ran across the smoothness of the bright plastic bowls, holding the fruit and vegetables, the bruised, rejected ones Maria brought home from the market. Within the pattern of the vibrant orange and purple curtains was a comfort knowing his mum had carefully cut, sewn, and hung them during his babyhood. The repetitive whirr of the treadle on the old Singer sewing machine could still lullaby him to sleep. He traced stories of faraway lands in the grain of the wood of the high stools, crafted by his father, one each for him and Emiliano, so they could sit up and reach the table, their legs swinging to the heartbeat of innocence.

Each day as Maria bustled around the kitchen he would fiddle with the frayed edges of the tablecloth, picking at the cotton strands. Each day he rehearsed in his head different ways of asking her to cut him a slice of bread, knowing he was trapped in a never-ending struggle in his tiny, compact seven-year-old body. Faced with so many challenges to his small stature and undeveloped sense of self, survival felt like the best he could hope for. *But don't let mum know*, he constantly reminded himself. *Don't add to her worries.*

'Mum, I really like the way you slice the bread, could

you do it for me this morning?'

'Mum, my wrist is aching this morning, would you cut the bread for me today please?'

'Mum, can you show me how you cut the bread so I can get better at doing it for myself?'

But however much he practised, he was unable to find the words that might not arouse her suspicions, might get Emiliano into trouble and himself into even greater trouble later when his brother would serve out his revenge with bitter unpredictability.

At exactly eight o'clock Maria left, carefully closing the wooden door behind her, trapping the early heat of the day outside and the still, stagnant remains of the night-time inside, the kitchen curiously quiet after she left, as if more than one person had departed the room. Emilio, an all too familiar knot in his stomach, looked across the table at his brother. *Please brother, not the same torment today. Please find some kindness towards me. I love you however you treat me, but please don't be hurtful.*

Emiliano, not meeting his brother's eye, began his daily routine: he picked up the bread knife and with slow, smooth strokes sliced through its crust. Each stroke released a mouth-watering yeasty aroma. Emilio squeezed his eyes shut, wanting, yearning to suppress the rising tears, the salty stinging tears of vulnerability. Unrelenting Emiliano cut the crusty bookend off the loaf and placed it on his own plate. Next, he cut another slice with exaggerated slowness and laid that next to the crust. Emilio knew that if he spoke, a torrent of sadness might pour from his mouth, which would then unleash a physical punishment from his twin. Silence was the better option—marginally better, less confrontational. Maybe by hiding deep within his silence he could pretend these scenarios were not happening. Maybe it would all just stop.

Emiliano placed the bread knife perpendicular to the loaf on the edge of the breadboard. Picking up the butter knife (never had a rounded blade appeared such an object of menace in the hands of a child), he cut a sliver off the edge of the butter and spread it with smooth precise movements onto his crust. And then the jam, lovingly made by Maria from strawberries grown in terracotta pots in their garden. He stuck the knife deep into the luscious, sticky sweetness, contaminating it with crumbs, lifting a large dollop from the jar onto his bread and spreading it on top of the butter, making sure, with mathematical precision, it reached the edges of the bread. *Maybe, just maybe this time he is preparing this with tender care for me; maybe I have misjudged him,* thought the silent spectator.

Emilio smoothed crumbs from the tablecloth with his good hand, trembling as he pressed out creases in the cotton, still trying to keep control over the accumulating tears threatening to spill over his cheeks like a dam breaking under the pressure of a long, long spell of rain. He bit the inside of his lip. His brother took the carefully prepared crust in his right hand, raised his eyes to look directly at Emilio and, after licking his lips with the flamboyance of a street mime artist, bit into it.

'Delicious,' he said. Emilio sat placidly, consciously rubbing his thumb stump with his left hand.

*

School was a similar canvas on which Emiliano could

paint the same brotherly image he had concocted for Maria's eyes—he as the protector twin, the one without the disability, who could be relied upon to help his weaker brother. The overstretched teachers, overstretched by voluable, spirited children, high in numbers and higher in energy, welcomed this help. Emilio, they resigned, was probably never going to write as the absence of his right thumb made holding a pencil or crayon impossible: the whole acceptance of left-hand dominance was still a generation away. So all that was expected of Emilio in the classroom was for him to be biddable, to cause no nuisance and make his spiritual presence as tiny as his physical presence. Emiliano meanwhile blossomed, producing line upon line of beautifully even, repeated letters, rapidly escalating from a pencil to the accolade of being permitted to write by pen:

ddddddddddddddddddddddddddddddddd
eeeeeeeeeeeeeeeeeeeeeeeeeeeeeeeeeeeeeeeeeeeeeee
ffffffffffffffffffffffffffffffffffffffffffffff

Little gold and silver stickers of praise twinkled across his workbook, like stars in a clear night sky, while Emilio produced a spider web of angular lines, as much as clutching the pencil between his first and middle finger would allow, his knuckles whitening from the pressure. 'Maybe he will be an artist, maybe farm the land, maybe work behind the counter of a local grocery store,' the teacher gently suggested to Maria, each knowing, but not acknowledging, this would be an unlikely route to help him escape the clutches of a village in decline—a village unable to compete with the opportunities of the city.

I am clever; in my head, I am clever. I know I am. At least as clever as my twin.

Emilio, sitting on his hands, muttered the answer to any sum the teacher called out before any classmate could even raise their hand; his imagination sparkled and fizzed, inventing fantasy lands and fantastic stories. But for now, he needed to wait for another two decades to fully accept that going into battle with his brother would always leave him on the losing side. He just needed to learn the patience of how to bide his time and believe that the universe would one day turn in his favour.

*

In the blink of Maria's eye, life moved forwards. Her sons became too large to be considered children, yet too small to be fully fledged men.

Overall, teenage life in their village was boring. Emiliano spent hours lying on his narrow child's bed, tucked under the eaves in the airless top floor bedroom, counting the days until he could be let loose into the wide world. His mind would wander and wonder, a never-ending refrain of rattling resentment. 'Why can't Mum buy me things like the other boys have?' All his eyes could see as he surveyed his slumped body was a rattle bag outfit—a faded green tie dye t-shirt, scratchy next to his skin, the fibres having been laundered into submission. His beige trousers had been designed for a child in the military style of fashion popular ten years ago, while his sweater would be so, so embarrassing were it not that it's chevron pattern had recently and inexplicably become stylish. Why for once could he not have clothes, which arrived in fresh packaging from the city stores and were ahead of fashion trends, rather than items handed down from other village families? He wanted clothes that fitted his bandied legs and short arms, rather than always having to squeeze himself into lurid jolly clothes designed for an average six-year-old. He wanted football boots. He wanted a bike, or at least a skateboard; either would bridge his access into the cool group of his peers. He wanted, he wanted—he wanted not to be himself.

Maria was trying; she toiled to the brink of exhaustion day after day. When she was not working on her market stall, she was busy with housework; when she was not helping their elderly neighbours run errands to the pharmacy, the baker, the market, she baked for the village spring fete. The wheel of work and housework turned faster than she could keep pace with. *Oh to be a better mother! Oh to be a better neighbour! Oh to just be enough!* The ever-deepening lines on her forehead and telling insomniac's pallor challenged the beauty of her youth. Some days it was too hard to keep everything going.

When Maria called him for supper for the third time, Emiliano stomped down the wooden stairs to the kitchen, refusing to meet her eye as she greeted him, refusing to acknowledge her weariness after a long day standing in the market. The only sound over their meal was forks chasing tortilla around plates and the heavy gulping silence being swallowed, until finally Emiliano glared at Maria and said, in a tone slightly harsher than even his long-held resentment intended: 'When is Dad coming back?'

Not now, please not now, I just don't have the energy to deal with all this, thought his wearisome mother. She carefully laid down her fork, her meal barely touched. 'He is not, my darling boy. You must realise now after two years since he left that he has built himself a new life without us across the valley.'

'But he'd come back if you asked him, or if you just made yourself look prettier and stopped wearing those frumpy dresses and dull shoes, and combed your hair properly.'

Cutlery was thrown down onto the table with a tympanic crash of anger at the unfairness of the world. Maria rose from her chair, pretending to busy herself by prematurely washing dishes from their unfinished meal; her back was turned on her son as she blinked away tears. She was too tired for this today, as she had been last week and last year. But as always, she would continue to pour her love into him day after day, ignoring his rebounding frustration and being led by her maternal intuition keeping the channels to her heart open, ready for when, as she believed, he would be willing to return. And she would then welcome him home with the unconditional forgiveness only mothers can fully comprehend.

*

Maddox High School sat in the morning shadow of the volcano. Tiny fragments of volcanic dust floated in the classroom air, too small to be seen with the pupils' eyes, but large enough to linger as a putrid smell penetrating the teenage twin's lungs; their breath, shallow and grasping, creating a constant low-level anxiety. Emilio had by now additional angst, the years with an unpredictable twin accumulating, worrying away at his central nervous system. This conscious ploy by Emiliano kept him perpetually on guard, manifesting in many ways, which got more and more elaborate as the years provided him opportunities to perfect the techniques of passive aggression. Sometimes his brother's attack would be simple and straightforward: removing Emilio's homework from his school backpack just before it was due to be handed to the teacher; or ferreting into his brother's gym bag and tying the laces of his plimsolls like a gordian knot, knowing it would be a mighty struggle for Emilio to untie before class. At other times the attack would be more calculated: Emiliano would line his brother up for future admonishments by volunteering him for roles he would be unable to perform—a role in the school swimming team, carrying art easels to the top floor studio, or he would imitate his laboured handwriting in a love note hidden inside a girl's desk, evoking her mocking scorn in front of their classmates.

Despite, or perhaps because of all this agitation, Emilio located an inner calm, buried deep within his solar plexus. The attacks came from his mirror image, literally his other half, yet they were not of him. He looked outward, to see life beyond where his own emotions began and ended. He learned empathy. Empathy especially for Maria. The boy begins to become the man, the child to become the parent. None of this was his mother's fault, yet all of it was her burden. Outwardly strong, inwardly kind, and gentle, she should be sheltered from the consequences of his and Emiliano's short stature—from the poverty, loneliness, and mostly the judgements. The judgements that pervaded their lives, in ever proximity. Diego, their neighbour, a surly, solitary man with a damaged soul, took every chance to voice opinions as harsh as his face creased with anger—in the café, in the bar, on his own doorstep—wherever he could garner an audience. 'Have you watched Maria's boys? Their bodies are small, yet they take up space wherever they go. They should know their place. And why aren't they more fun, they're too serious for my liking—after all they are always going to be kids aren't they?'

The men he supped beer with were compliant. Merely raising glasses to their mouths, and watching the twins walk by, nodding like ciphers devoid of their own opinions.

Where and when the twins located their commonality, however, was as teenagers. They both found steel in their bellies—the languorous days of acned adolescence, succumbing to darkened masturbatory bedrooms was not for them. Beyond the rush of early testosterone, their belief, not yet conscious to them, was that with enough self-will they could realign the configuration of the stars on the night of their birth and be born anew. Maybe it is easier to catch a cloud in a jam jar than for us to rewrite our fate, but each of them was damned sure they would try. After all, what did they have to lose?

Four

'Ladies and gentlemen. Amigos y amigas. Now for the highlight of the evening's show.'

The house lights dimmed. The spotlight roved menacingly around the auditorium and the crowd squealed in anticipation until it landed in the centre, the mandala, the ring, dusted with chalk and flanked by worn, fraying ropes. Cheers went up. The master of ceremonies, dapper in his shiny black shirt with scarlet red tie, stepped into this spotlight, arms in the air as if victory was already his. In a caricature of machismo, the sweat stains of his armpits mirrored by the glossiness of his moustache. One trouser leg was hooked nonchalantly over the top of his dusty ankle boot, which looked suspiciously two sizes too large for his foot. Lucha libre had come to town.

Cheers resounded, bouncing off the walls in a maelstrom. An all-female mariachi band paraded in single file, beating out a pulsing rhythm of expectation, sashaying in single file among the crowd. Their outfits of russet and gold satin caught and reflected light shafts intruding from the skylight in kaleidoscopic fractals. They played with infectious joy, uninhibited smiles beneath broad-brimmed straw hats. The crowd echoed the beat, hands clapping, feet stomping. Most wore masks imitating their heroes; stretched satin with eyes and mouth holes to see and breathe through. Turquoise and purple and orange and midnight blue. A lurid, vibrant sea of colour—a mixture of miniature comic book superheroes and underdressed matadors in search of angry bulls.

'I bring for you El Cuate Corona. Our technicos.'

The crowd erupted, whooping, clapping, and whistling as a tall figure dressed from head to toe in black, adorned with the luminous bones of the human skeleton, parted the crowd, and strutted to the ring. His right-hand held Emilio's left and his left-hand Emiliano's right, as if guiding them back from the underworld like a numinous figment.

These shorts are too tight tonight, thought Emilio, conscious of how snugly they fitted below his protruding belly. *Folks don't care though; it's just me. Why is the elastic digging in? Have they shrunken in the wash? I can't pull them up or even down a bit, can't destroy the illusion, can't appear too much of a human. Keep smiling through the mask, through the sequins, the light-dancing sequins.* Looking at his brother in contrasting black-and-silver mask through which Emiliano's eyes were only just visible, he broke into a genuine smile, assured that each of them was majestic with their swirling capes draped over their shoulders, accentuating their hairless, oiled chests. *Look at us—here in the spotlight, finally the spotlight. Perfect!*

On arrival at the ringside, the Skeleton bent down and lifted each luchador in turn. In swift movements the twins each vaulted the ropes and ran recklessly, backflipping and cartwheeling, giving the audience the spectacle they desired—wrestlers with the strength of men and the reckless playfulness of youth.

It was Friday night. The week's work was truly behind the crowd; the weekend stretched like a languid cat on a summer's day. Welcoming the air rank with the aroma of cheap cigars, fried corn, and testosterone-imbibed sweat, they breathed in this interlude of freedom. The few women in the seats made their presence felt with cheap, cloying perfume. The floor was sticky with spilt beer as people clambered unapologetically over each other's legs to their seats. A troupe of other wrestlers, some yet to fight, others feeling the adrenaline-elation of their match done, gathered on a raised platform to spectate.

With impeccable timing, the master of ceremonies waited until the wave of noise just subsided and then raised his arms once more, ready to evoke another crescendo. 'Ladies and gentlemen. Amigos y amigas. I bring to you our rudos.'

Well-rehearsed in the rules of this carnival, the crowd, en masse, like an aroused, untamed beast, broke into spitting hisses, stamping in a raggedy rhythm, soundwaves gradually equalising into a menacing beat, as two unusually tall men strode from the parted purple velvet curtains of the changing rooms. A few steps, each planted with deliberation like giants pacing a mythical forest, transported them to the ringside. Gold leotards clung to their frames: wide, muscular shoulders, colossus legs and rounded bellies which they thumped in imitation of a bestial mating call. One wore a mask of red and green satin while the other's was burnished orange. Small-pupiled eyes stared out, darting, defying the crowd not to disrespect them.

The twins looked out from the ring with exaggerated frowns on furrowed foreheads straining beneath their masks, exchanged looks of trepidation as their opponents strutted the perimeter of the ring gladiatorially, their heads jutting from thick necks in an aggressive challenge. On the second row of the audience seats, a small boy broke into sobs of terror and buried his face behind his father's arm.

Emiliano adored the spectacle of anticipation, the heady adrenaline surging through his body—oh the deliciousness of it all! The delight of the spectacle! When faced with the decision of fight or flight, fight would always be his choice. *It would be great, so bloody great to take that winner's belt home to Mum, to make her proud of me just for once.* Despite their constant invitations and pleading, she always excused herself from her boys' matches on the pretence of an endless supply of housework. Conspiratorially, all three held their silence, aware of her fear of witnessing her boys being subject to the threats and violence from muscled men twice their size.

Slow inhale, longer exhale. Emilio slowed his breathing. Four in, eight out. It was not his opponents who unnerved him; the technicos had faced them several times in the past and were well-versed in their tactics. The loyalty amongst the wrestling troupe ran as deep and solid as unmined gold: whatever was performed for the audience's delight, beneath the public spectacle of the fights they were bonded as only a tribe of social misfits can be. To society they were freaks and punks—to each other they were a family. It was his true blood brother, his twin, who was the source of his anxiety. *Can I trust him to rescue me if the match takes a turn against us?* Their timing needed to be in perfect synchronicity, their thoughts in perfect harmony. Any chink would be spotted, seized and exploited by the rudos. He adjusted his mask, turning his head from side to side to rid his neck of the tightness where mask met flesh. Then he glanced over at Emiliano, trying to catch his eye. His twin studiously looked away from him into the back of the crowd. Emilio adjusted his mask again.

The scene was set, the lights dimmed, and a crash of cymbals heralded the arrival of the great arbitrator—the referee. His hair slicked back, Elvis-like. In his zebra-striped top, he ran athletically in an unathletic body and slid seamlessly under the bottom rope to enter the ring with a flourish, usually the preserve of kings and princes. He stood erect—stern and serious, seemingly oblivious to the loud 'Ooooooh' coming from the crowd.

The crowd's foot stomping continued. There, over there, stationed on the west side of the ring, Emilio spotted a large group of the twins' supporters; it was curious to witness them mirrored back at him, a crowd wearing identical masks as himself and Emiliano. There they stood as a motley collective of vagabonds and ne'er-do-wells with mean bodies and kind eyes, vicariously living through the drama and risk, living in the margins, in the shadows. The underdog supporting the underdog. What this troupe lacked in conventionality they made up for with fierce loyalty.

The referee stood precisely in the centre of the ring, feet planted firmly on the wrestling insignia reproduced on the floor. With a raised arm, as if quelling a rising ocean, he quietened the crowd to the calmness of a millpond, ready to swell into a tsunami at the smallest provocation.

'Tonight, we have the match to outclass all others.

Nothing, like nothing has gone before. We are going to see our smallest but fiercest technicos take on the vicious giant rudos. What will win out, size or agility? Muscle or skill?'

An eruption of cheering, hissing, whooping, and whistling ensued along with a communal release of excitement. The surging energy of the crowd, present enough to be touched and tasted.

The rudos snarled like bulldogs straining at leashes, the embodiment of all that threatens the social order—symbols of misrule and the criminal underclass. Sometimes drug dealers, sometimes thieves and vandals. Sometimes the bank manager. The rudos were bullies, out to show how thuggery could dominate. Facing them were the technicos, the goodies—the cops to the robbers, the light to the dark—there to show how those on the side of the gods would always conquer. The crowd dutifully divided their loyalties in a simple, binary way—this side or that one—good or bad—obedience or rule breakers. Those who lived life guided by a strong moral compass were freed up for one evening to cheer for the darkness without consequence, like children who secretly hope the wolf will eat up grandma.

Emilio knew a degree of humiliation was the price he must pay, the entertainment quota of the public sport. *If I close my mind, if tight, tight shut, if I sell my soul I could do it. It's what they want, what they pay their ticket price for—to see us perform.* He tumbled with his brother. They rolled and ran amok, imitating the unpredictability of toddlers after a birthday party fuelled by excess candy and cake. Emiliano, less conscious, less concerned by such ethical dilemmas, took to the ring, positioning himself by the rope opposite his brother eager and ready to tag. The rudos limbered up with fiery looks, an exchanged whisper about tactics and a dusting of chalk to their hands, spreading like tightly bunched bananas. A percussive clatter. The bell heralded the commencement of the match.

This was what the twins had trained for. This is where their unity lay. Their early mornings at the practice ring had been in anticipation of this moment: their chance to show the world that although small in stature, they were huge in skill and athleticism. Born with fate's scales tipped against them, they rose above through sheer grit and determination. A role model for every child of this country. The making of a national hero. The making of two national heroes.

Emilio watched with an eye trained like a tiger's keeper. *Keep focused, keep focused.* His brother made a small gesture with his right hand resting on his lower back, just below the elastic of his shorts, displaying to him the comparative agility of his right-hand thumb. Emilio's heartbeat retreated from the tympanic noise inside his inner ear—four breaths in, eight out—yet there was not enough time—two in, four out—*don't get distracted.* The match didn't start with the bell, but with this signal between them, a secret message: *I have your back. Calm, calm, we are a team. In this sacred arena we are a team, the two of us against the world. For now.* Emilio raised himself up onto tiptoe, stretched his chest over the second rope and roared: 'Le mata hermaro! Kill him brother!'

*

Hot and sticky Lillibet sat in the only bearable place, outdoors in Consuelo's yard. Cicadas marked their dusk tango beat as she, Pilar, and Eva shelled nuts for her mother. The sun bowed its head below the volcano rim, drawing back the last shadow of the day's scene so familiar to the three young women, friends since young girls. For Lillibet, it was meditative: she could let herself go. Embrace the comfort it afforded. The three young women squatted with strong thighs on low wooden stools forming three points of a triangle, their skirts hitched above their knees, each with a metal bucket between their feet into which they dropped the newly shod cashews while throwing the shells into the communal bucket at their centre. Each had hair pulled into long plaits thrown back, absorbing some of the sweat from their shoulder blades. Theirs was an easy companionship, and although still in their twenties, they knew their friendship not only stretched backwards into their short histories, but reached forward into beckoning futures. Just like those of their mothers, whose bonds had transcended the years of marriage, miscarriage and mourning and were now focused on menopause and the slow movement of time. Lillibet was the first to break the easy stillness between the women.

'It is not enough, is it? Being "allowed" in shops and clubs is only giving us what the mestizos have. Surely, we should hope for more?'

Ping, ping the refrain of nutshell against metal bucket as the young cholitas fell into an easy rhythm.

'Oh Lillibet, you're never satisfied.' An audible sigh came from Pilar. 'We already have so much more than our mothers. We should accept that, be grateful, or the shopkeepers, club owners, and gym guys will take it away from us again.'

'I won't let them,' said Lillibet, as she sat upright on her stool, pulling her shoulders back and down. 'If they think they can take away my independence, they will have a shock coming to them!'

Pilar gave a small snort but kept her eyes down. 'Six months at the gym, pumping some iron and you think you're as strong as any man?'

'I'm not talking only about physical strength,' Lillibet fired back, 'I'm also talking about my inner strength—my soul. I have a fire in my belly no one can extinguish. But if you want to talk about muscles, look at these.' She pushed back her shawl and grabbed at the sleeves of her blouse, flexing well-toned biceps.

'Tsk,' hissed Pilar, 'Call those muscles lady?'

Lillibet, conflicted between affection and annoyance, stood to challenge her friend. 'I can take you on any time you like. I'll show you what my muscles can do.'

'Fine come on then, bring it on!' said Pilar as she stood, extending her neck to increase her height. They met eye to eye, nose to nose, soul to soul. With hands on each other's shoulders, grasping cloth and flesh, they swayed left to right, foot to foot, like mating crabs. A fuse, dry for years, had been lit by barely a spark. Friends became rivals. The gravel underfoot skittered, dust stuck to their skirts. Momentum gathered, their movements a tarantella, spinning faster and faster. In a small stumble, Lillibet kicked aside one of the metal buckets, scattering nutshells haywire across the yard.

The two friends shifted their weight from left to right, pushing harder onto each other's shoulders. Eva, always the pacifier, compelled to watch, confused at the turn the evening had taken, sprang out of their way. Frowning beneath her heavy monobrow, she gathered up her skirt, rapidly rescuing stools, and the remaining bucket, clearing the path so emotions could escape. 'Please, please don't. Just calm down both of you, you'll hurt each other.' Her quiet pleas inaudible.

The two friends, locked like matador and bull, sensing the parameters of their space when nearing the beds of geraniums and neat rows of beans, swung back into the spotlight cast by a hanging lamp.

They danced, fought. They sweated, moaned. Neither prepared to relinquish power in this battle, a strength they did not know they possessed rising in each of them. All the years of restraint in the face of public scorn had built wills of iron within their cores into which they now hunkered down. They each flashed dark, deep-pooled eyes at each other. *I love you, but I will beat you down.*

As the spectacle danced over onto the circular, dried out yellow and brown lawn, Consuelo, on hearing the commotion, came running from the kitchen, gripping her tea towel between arthritic fingers. 'Girls, girls, what on earth are you doing! Stop this at once! This is not who you are!' Eva looked at her with pleading eyes, hoping Consuelo's age and wisdom might know better than her how to intervene.

As Pilar glanced around, a momentary lapse in her concentration brought by glimpsing their enlarged shadows cast by the moon was all Lillibet needed. She seized it, and catching her opponent off balance, hooked her left leg behind Pilar's right and pushed her backwards. Pilar fell with an expression of wide surprise on her face, her shoulders hitting the earth first closely followed by her hips then head. She crumpled like a deflating accordion. The clock's hands froze as Lillibet lost her balance and, in slow motion, fell on top of her friend with a flourish of taffeta, petticoat and sweet sweat, displacing the humid air. There was too much of her, too much weight, too much energy coursing her veins, now the fight had been brought to a thudding halt.

'Tssk!' cried the winded Pilar, as she used her last ounce of strength to push Lillibet off her. The fight was over, and to the sound of their heavy breaths, they lay side by side like lovers when passion is spent. Neither uttered a word, they just lay there, trying to recover physically and emotionally. Neither noticed the bloody scratches they had given and received. What had just passed between them? A small part of both knew it was wrong, but a much larger part knew it was right. And they knew that each other knew this. Something had been awakened that couldn't be quenched—they had crossed a threshold. La Ciguapa, the feral woman, had been set loose and would destroy whoever tried to block her path.

As their breathing calmed and synchronised, Lillibet reached out her right hand, taking hold of Pilar's left. And there they both lay, as still as a pair of moon-bathing sloths, feeling the pulse of mother earth beneath them, looking up into a dark blue sky lit with radiant stars. The ether had been disrupted and realigned; an energy put in motion and the spaces within their souls expanded, each in unison. Set alight like the passion of lovers—now they needed to unite it into a fireball of energy and unleash this on an unsuspecting world. It was time for the cholitas to rise up.

*

I'm sorry. I'm not sorry. I don't know what happened, but I feel better. Lillibet, before arriving in the kitchen, knew breakfast the following morning would be a sombre affair. By eight o'clock, her father had departed for work, taking her younger brother along to teach him the ways of the trade, intending to infuse him with a love of carpentry. He would show him the beauty of walnut and how its dark grain could be coaxed into soft curves, how the bark from the almond tree would snap if not soaked to suppleness.

Lillibet and Consuelo remained—just the mother and daughter alone in the kitchen, the morning air still and torpid from the rising sun rays trapped within the wooden door frames and shuttered door. Consuelo, restless through the humid night, had risen before sunset and attempted to rub her worries away by plunging hands into hot soapy water and rubbing, rubbing, rubbing cloth against suds, like a mantra. Her cuticles, already fragile from housework, now broken and sore in the hot water. Petticoats were subsequently dancing recklessly on the washing line, scarlet, emerald and kingfisher blue, prayer flags catching wishes in the wind.

When the empanadas and eggs were served onto chunky ceramic plates and the strong steaming coffee poured into thick handled mugs, there was no remaining activity mother and daughter could use to dance around the awkwardness between them. Consuelo was resigned, wearisome; her daughter, an unbiddable child, from an early age would not be easily moulded. This girl was going to carve her own path in the world's world, which would bend to her, not her to it, The energy of their volcanic landscape coursed through her veins, and as a mother she wondered to what extent she had encouraged this. In days past, her husband had been drawn to Consuelo's strength, like iron filings detecting a magnetic field; he had found little choice but to surrender to this attraction, despite contrary cries from his logical mind. Was the fire in the girls' belly a manifestation of hers—the one she had never allowed? But, witnessing Lillibet's performance last night, had she set her daughter on a track which had more momentum than the world was ready for? Lillibet was like the mint plant in her garden—either struggling at the constraints of the terracotta pot that could barely contain it, or, if planted in the ground, spreading and sucking nutrients out of more placid adjacent plants.

She had hoped a contrite, rested girl would rise from her bed this morning, but as soon as she sensed Lillibet's energy approaching the kitchen through their narrow entrance hall, she knew the opposite was the case—the girl had broken out beyond the bounds of her human body, her presence wider than her hips and higher than the curve of her bowler hat. She roared without a sound slipping through her lips—she was a brewing tornado in human form, with the wind giving rise to her fury. And for that Consuelo knew that while she partly feared for her daughter, she mostly envied her. Primarily, however, she was this girl's mother, and so advice, albeit unsolicited and undesired, was called for.

'Lillibet, child, are you ready to explain yourself now? What on earth do you think you were doing behaving in that way with Pilar last night?"

Maybe maternal love would shine through the preparation of food, soften this exchange?

'Do you want eggs with your coffee?'

Lillibet met her eyes with force, 'I don't understand the issue. And no, I don't want eggs.' A long pause... 'Thank you.'

'It's just not like you, pushing your Pilar around like that.'

'She was pulling while I was pushing. You make it sound as if it was all one-way.'

'But you started it.'

'You started it!' quipped back Lillibet. 'Have you heard yourself Mum, you sound like a toddler!'

'Don't speak to me like that. I'm your mother!'

Lillibet hesitated before her next response, a tallow was being lit, it needs quenching before it sucked in enough oxygen to become an inferno. She sat up ramrod straight on her stool, inhaling what little air was left in the room. 'I need more mum. I'm only going to live once, I only have this one life and I want it to count. I'm not as easily satisfied with the boring humdrum day in day out as you are.'

The knife entered Consuelo's tender heart. *Am I not enough? What I've provided for this girl, what I've sacrificed, still not enough. Why is it never enough for her?* She prided herself on her resilience, having weathered years as a cholita, revisiting the hostile gazes in the shops, the taunts on the streets, always an outsider, but now all she wanted was to lie down alone, in a cool, quiet room and sleep, sleep, sleep.

Petulant now, resenting her mother for deflating her newly unfurled sails and pointing her back in the direction of a safe but suffocating shore, Lillibet rubbed the quick from her fingernails and uttered, more softly, 'I just need more mum. I just need more.'

It was fruitless to argue further. Consuelo could recognise determination when she saw it. 'Well then, we'd better teach you how to fight properly, so that you don't get hurt, then,' answered Consuelo, holding her daughter's stare until a contagious smile broke the lock for both, neither knowing who had cracked first.

All events in our lives build upon something that preceded it, and we can never be separated from the backward pull and forward thrust of history. But at that very moment, Lillibet knew this was a beginning, the newest of new beginnings. This was the point that later, looking back, she would pinpoint as when her passion for wrestling began.

*

When the folks who arrived to 'discover' this land felt that the glorious mountains, volcanoes, verdant valleys, and terraces leading the rocky path to the sea's edge were not enough, they built an observatory to enable them to expand their curiosity and desire to capture into outer space and to bequeath names to the stars. Little did they realise that their real need was to look inwards, not further and further out. But that, and the chasm between what we think we need and what we need, is another story.

Although the adventurers left a trail of destruction and resentment, they also left a whole lot of telescopes, enough to populate an observatory. A wealthy but anonymous local benefactor bequeathed enough money in his will to allow the observatory to stay open and therefore enable the townsfolk to star gaze for decades thereafter. These townsfolk were never sure if the benefactor's intention was for them to have broad, ambitious horizons, or to forever feel keenly their small and insignificant presence in the universe.

The observatory on the hill was open every day, apart from each 13th of March, as specified in the rich benefactor's will. Although the gift was anonymous, the ego and the childlike desire for his day of birth to be forever remembered, would always win out in some way.

Entry was free. Why then did Lillibet and Pilar feel compelled to break in on certain evenings once the chitter-chattering children and their worldweary parents had departed for home and bedtime stories. Stargazing women with their feet on the ground. The two young women loved to do this once the night sky was dark, and illumination came from the planets rather than sunlight. Lillibet wondered how far away these constellations were and if they could hear songs from each other; her friend believed in the silence and vastness.

Two evenings after what would forever be known as 'the yard episode,' the two women, once again bonded in friendship, forced the observatory side door by taking turns to push slowly with their shoulders until it sighed open in submission. Pilar's neighbour, Niels, had been the caretaker here longer than their memories could stretch. He had always seemed like an elderly man, having become sullen and prematurely serious since the shock of sudden illness and consequent passing of a wife who had always been too beautiful, too fragile for him. Lillibet and Pilar would regularly sit on Consuelo's doorstep at the cooling point of the day when dogs were waking from their prolonged siestas, pretending to chat to passers-by in timeworn ways, while waiting for Niels to arrive home for his long, lonely nights. *Quick, quick, Pilar he's home, the coast is clear.* The observatory was once again unsupervised, fair game.

This evening they clattered up the wrought iron circular staircase, taking steps two at a time, raised petticoats in their hands. Arriving under the domed glass ceiling, they threw themselves down, the full weight of their bodies succumbing to the support of the freshly swept floor.

'Wait, wait, Lillibet, our eyes will adjust to the dark, we just must be a little patient. Wait and it happens by magic." And sure enough their focus shifted from the nearness of the everyday human shapes, doorknobs and ticket stubs to a vast focus of the far, far away solar system.

'See now, the constellations begin to twinkle. We can see in the dark!' In hushed tones they indulged their favourite sport, as the stars winked encouragement on them like benevolent grandparents, the two young women bequeathed them names.

'There, look there, can you see our warrior prince? No, more to the left and up a bit. You can see his bow hand pulling back, ready to release the arrow into the beating hearts of our enemies.' Lillibet traced a pattern across the sky with her index finger, bracelets rippling and tinkling against each other.

'And up there to the right is the virgin,' exalted Pilar.

'How do you know she's a virgin?'

'She is smaller than the others. I think she's trying not to be noticed.'

'Can you see our pomegranate tree? I can't see it tonight?'

'No, I can't. It must be resting its branches now. We will just need to imagine the pomegranate seeds bursting fresh and succulent on our tongues.'

'Shh now, it's time for us to count how many stars are watching us, watching them tonight.'

And so they lay quietly, each trying to quantify the universe, until Lillibet whispered to her friend, 'Pilar, do you think the earth is as vast as the sky out there? Do you think there are places we can ever find where our hearts can rest and be content?'

'Yes, I do. But we must go there together, so neither of us is lost and drifts where no one will find us, like baby seahorses who swim the oceans in search of their lost mothers.'

'And to do this,' whispered Lillibet out into the never-ending sky, 'we must make peace with Pachamama, we must carry her in our hearts to keep us connected to this land.'

They lay in peace, imagining Mother Earth's heart beating beneath that vain domed construction. A pact was made, an uncertain course set in motion, and they joined the lesser-known realms of intrepid women explorers who set their aim not to conquer others, but to lead them towards new possibilities.

*

When Lillibet first ventured, wrestling was not considered a ladylike sport. Not then. That space belonged to men as much as smoky afternoon cafés, where the local men whiled away languid afternoons with jovial games of backgammon, strong black coffee and Metaxa.

If you were to venture into local community halls on a Friday evening, you would smell testosterone, these places of refuge where menfolk flee the binds of domesticity when they feel tied too tightly. These places where each male village pup passes through the coveted portal, boy to man. Wives, girlfriends, and daughters have been schooled not to enter, not to invade; should there be an emergency, an elderly parent who falls, a child whose fever worsens, a fire unquenched by water buckets, and a man is needed back home, boys are sent on buried errands, over the threshold, to fetch fathers and husbands. Time past and present, the male species was always thus.

'Pah!' thought Lillibet. 'Who made these rules? Men of course! The same men who scorn my mother when she walks down the road in her petticoats. Nonsense!'

At seventeen, Lillibet didn't know her ambitions, but she was comfortable enough defining her future self by what she didn't want to be. She was too young, too unworldly to attribute this to an absence of role models who could show her possibilities, believe in her. Yet the next generation of role models must always start somewhere. Lillibet didn't set out consciously to be a pioneer; common sense just left her little choice.

The evening Lillibet stepped into the hall took courage, one she had built over years of growing impatience at the lack of social justice. And when courage calls loudly enough to our waiting hearts, we are compelled. And when this listening is no longer sufficient, we act.

'We're going to make history tonight girls.' She rallied her posse of friends with the boldness of youth. Sadly, they were merely reframing an ever-repeating history in a different time and place: the lone cowboy who walks into the bar in a strange town, the hillwalkers who enter the pub of locals at the bottom of the valley, or the awkward teenager who braves the party thrown by the cool set. The difference this time was that Lillibet was not an outsider in this town. Throughout her life she had barely ventured further than the echo of local gossip; everyone had known her since she was a tiny mewling babe. This town, its ways of living, were woven into the tapestry of her being. Tonight, however, she was an outsider—a woman entering the dominant world of men.

Lillibet and her friends had rehearsed this evening in their backyards for two weeks and consequently their choreography was perfect. As they stepped over the threshold, the plywood door, the green paint in much need of a refresh, a rumble of silence rippled around the room, pregnant with unspoken words. An expectant lull pervaded before surprise could be replaced by objection; the young women acted as one combined unit, a tiny army.

'We can do this,' Lillibet muttered to herself, swallowing the lump in her throat. *There is Miguel. We must move fast.* Within a blink the group shifted across the room in one smooth movement like a bride's silken wedding dress train. Forming a ring around their prey, containing him like a key in a pocket. His eyes darted from one of the young women to the other, and then occasionally beyond this small circle in attempts to catch the eyes of his peers, to call them to his rescue. These long-time friends of Miguel acted like a crumbling barrier studiously pretending to be in deep conversation, each with the other. There is safety in the pack even if it means sacrificing one singled out as a victim.

Miguel was unofficially the most respected man in the town. Those with official honours wore mayoral and judicial paraphernalia and sat in stuffy rooms deciding the destiny of their constituents, of whose day-to-day struggles and passions they understood little. But the person who held the real power, the respect of his neighbours, friends and acquaintances, was the wrestling trainer, Miguel. He had schooled, coached, and bullied his protégés into winning hallowed prizes in the ring. No one would publicly admit this, but the knowledge was held more sacred than evensong blessings. Miguel upheld the town's male pride. For the last twelve years his troupe had returned home victorious from regional competitions with the wrestling belt securely theirs, each victory heightening his status. He was known for working magic in cultivating strength and technique. What he lacked in stature he made up for in charisma. His past life before arriving here was a story he chose not to tell. Some speculated he had served time in prison having used his strength unwisely and immorally, and now, to seek redemption, was channelling his skills into good and glory for the young in body and ambitious in spirit. Others thought he was the product of an unpleasant, vicious divorce, and now immersed in the maleness of wrestling to no longer grapple with the complexities of women. In many respects he was a cipher on whom the locals could impose any story any given day. But the most important fact was his apparent celibacy, his abstinence in interest for women, men, or boys. Assuredly he was no threat to the menfolk, who he otherwise might cuckold, or to their sons who they feared might be defiled under his tutelage.

This evening he was the quarry the cholitas needed. If

they were going to wrestle, they were going to make damned sure they would be coached by him. There would be a challenge ahead of them and they wanted to amass as much strength in their corner as possible.

It was inevitable Lillibet, their queen bee, spoke first; precise, well-rehearsed. 'Miguel, we know how well-respected you are, not only by everyone who comes here every week, but by us too.'

Perspiration settled inside Miguel's collar, *Why are none of the windows in here open; the air was as torpid as treachery.*

'We have an opportunity for you,' she continued with a faked assuredness any commission-driven salesperson would envy. 'Me and the other girls are going to learn to wrestle, and we've chosen you as our coach and trainer.'

No reply from Miguel. How could he reply when he couldn't fit what he was hearing into his world map?

'We will come to you four times a week and we will be the best, most diligent students you've ever had. On the days we're not here we will be in the gym, pumping iron, building our strength.'

Miguel, managing to briefly gather himself, made a fool's mistake and began negotiating the details rather than challenging the premise. Lillibet and her friends exchanged looks, as fleeting as a poker player's tell. 'I know you girls don't have jobs, how can you possibly pay me? I'm not a charity here you know.'

'We understand,' interjected Pilar. 'What we will do is pay you 25% of any prize money for the next five years. If you train us well, you will soon be a rich man.'

Looking back at this moment three years later in the enviable position of hindsight, he still couldn't rationalise why he had agreed. But many of our best decisions are made with our guts not our heads, and Miguel's gut had rumbled and knotted with an unfamiliar hunger. Before that moment, he had not realised the ropes of familiarity of the new life he had created, rather than anchoring him in safety, held him down. The dark hairs on his muscular arms stood in a ripple, reversing from his shoulders to his wrists so powerfully he was sure it must be visible. There was something contagious within the spirit of these young women.

It would have been foolish for him to give away his illusion of authority, so with a shrug he told them: 'I will give it a go for one week. You will soon get bored and realise it requires so much more skill and strength than you will ever have and then we can stop this nonsense and you will return to your sewing or whatever you do. And keep your attire decent, girls, because you're not bringing those damned petticoats into my ring. Now move aside and let me get on with the serious side of my business.' Did he imagine it, or had he heard a click of heels echoing like a round of applause as he exited their trap?

There is nothing comparable to the succulent taste of victory, which lingers sweetly on the tongue. At that moment, Lillibet knew it was a flavour she enjoyed and was determined to get used to. She motioned for her friends to move aside and let Miguel out of his entrapment; the petticoat promise could wait another day to be won.

Five

Although they had begun their lives on opposite sides of the equator, there was a high degree of predictability Lillibet, Emilio and Emiliano were going to meet, and the circumstances were not difficult to predict. But what was less certain is how they would find connection in this fragmented world. If only that was as easy as finding the common ground between opposites—the yin and yang, the hot and cold, the laughter and the sorrow. But all three of our unsettled souls have a cornucopia of fractals within: it's going to take more than one wrestling bout to knock unity into them. The carnival of the wrestling ring is, however, not a bad place to start.

Emiliano and Emilio had commissioned new masks for this event, one green and the other turquoise; they no longer allowed Maria to stitch them, making the excuse they did not want to put upon her, take advantage of her. But all three knew the truth was more about the coveted status of the professionally made masks than about this faux consideration for her ageing arthritic fingers.

Lovingly packed inside Lillibet's stylishly logoed suitcase was her own new outfit; this was considerably more dramatic and expensive than the twins' tiny masks and trunks. For what better publicity for the fashion houses than to have their own cholita displaying their wares in an international wrestling tournament. Much negotiation had taken place, with Lillibet exerting her upper hand like a stage magician consulting his audience: should he saw his lady in half or not?

'I need to be sure the seams of my petticoat are tightly stitched and will withstand the strains of throws and lunges. The black felt of this hat isn't high enough quality—it must gleam under the spotlight—this dull felt just isn't good enough."

Lillibet's perfectionist streak pushed every boundary— the thread on her shawl had to be delicate and gossamer, fine yet strong like a tightrope pulled taut across a circus tent. The quest for precision, her attention to detail went on and on. Finally, with all her demands met, wrapped in purple tissue paper, her costume was placed inside her case, both she and the fashionistas knowing the moment she stepped into the spotlight the kingfisher blue taffeta petticoat beneath the vibrant orange skirt would set camera flashbulbs ablaze and their advertisers' cash tills ringing. What so many of her entourage failed to comprehend, however, was that it was not within Lillibet's heart to seek sponsorship deals and magazine front pages. She was not interested or willing to become a puppet of the media, which she considered was for the vain and foolish. For her it was simply about the wrestling—the power but not the glory.

People jostled into the hall at least an hour and a half before the show was due to start. Although it is tricky to pinpoint the moment when the show commenced, the spectacle was as much in the anticipation as the action in the ring. The doorway was a portal into another world where folks could be who they wanted to be, or more of who they truly were. It was an escape into something so much more delicious than real life.

The spectators were equally as flamboyant as the main event, a symbiotic co-dependence between adored and adoring. But, as on any menu, the starter must always know its place as a palate stimulator and should not upstage the main course.

To the left of the wrestling ring sat a young man, cautiously holding hands with his date; his gaze kept checking back to her for a reaction across her youth filled face. What was she feeling? Did she like him? Had his selection of activity for the evening been right? Her cheeks are flushed—is that a sign of pleasure, or discomfort? Is she too hot? Does she hate it here? Squeezing her hand in apology for his choice this evening out, he mentally vowed that if she consented to a subsequent date, he would book the restaurant table overlooking the fountain in the square and greet her with a single red rose.

Devotees wore masks in tribute to their wrestler heroes and although uncomfortable with scratchy seams and cheap fabric, they wore them with aplomb and took endless evidential photos—one for the family album! Several family groups shuffled together in price-saving shared seats. Ten-year-olds as excited as great aunts at christenings, and their older teenage siblings slouched deep in their seats refusing to answer any question from their parents with more than a monosyllable and a shrug.

And then there were the wrestling aficionados, who knew the sport. Money began to change hands on the back of predictions. Swaggering with wide legged gaits and puffed out chests, they jiggled coins in their trouser pockets and spat boasts of their 'insider knowledge.' As the sticky heat of the auditorium increased with the filing in of more and more sweating bodies, so too did their bravado and adrenaline—like human shock absorbers they felt the vibration of the crowd first so the anticipatory wrestlers backstage could remain in relative calm.

The final ingredient in the crowd were the wildcards—it was impossible to tell if they were part of the act or eccentrics: the two tall nuns with hairy hands, wearing large wooden crosses over wimples; the short, stout, bald man dressed in the zebra-stripe shirt of a referee; the old dowager who took up her solitary seat on the front row, getting in everyone's way with her wooden walking stick. And Maria and Juan Carlos, who sat stock still, hands in their laps, like the weather people in a cuckoo clock, surprised to find themselves both simultaneously out in public and exposed in the open. Although silent, the air between them was heavy with unspoken questions and betrayed promises like a widow's heart. They were out of place in their worn, dated clothes and in a relationship clearly beyond its sell by date. The mutual love for their boys overrode their own discomfort, however. But anyone who lingered long enough to look closely in their eyes, would notice their apparent disorientation. How had lives, once on predictable, safe trajectories, capitulated into this strange, jangly, sticky place?

Lillibet had nearly lost her nerve at least eight times. Not being a person prone to episodes of anxiety, she decided to stop counting as she realised it was beginning to take her down an uncomfortable route of obsessive observation. Instead, she concentrated on steadying her nerves. Because she had always appeared so outwardly confident, almost to the point of brashness, no elder had taught her the skills for which she was now in much need. She tidied the caravan's kitchen and then tidied it again, making sure every pot, piece of cutlery, and condiment was in its rightful place. Each item was under her control, behaving itself. Intuitively she took deep diaphragmatic breaths every time she felt the heat of an undermining thought rising. It would be decades until the term 'imposter syndrome' entered the common lexicon, but that merely meant the sensations hadn't yet been named, not that they did not exist, a kaleidoscope of sharp shards ready to deflate confidence. Most things in the world have been there for years, decades or even centuries before someone can label and usually then monetise it. Lillibet's sense that she did not belong and worse still would be rumbled, exposed, or humiliated in public, was common among women pioneers' way before they invaded boardrooms, and way before they learned to lean in.

Where was Pilar? Why had she disappeared just when Lillibet needed her calming presence? Her never-ending encouragement, her gentle mood music for the last few years had gone walkabout. Her anchor was missing. For now, she only had two competing voices to contend with inside her head:

Lillibet I: *This is what you've trained for—all those hours with Miguel. All that time in the gym. All the early mornings and late nights. It is what you wished for.*

Lillibet II: *But after all, Miguel is just a local guy—what does he know about this international scene? It is on a whole new level—big, really big.*

Lillibet I: *It is all about you now girl, not Miguel.*

Lillibet II: *Exactly, it is all about me now. Just me here on my own with hundreds of people out there expecting to be entertained. Sweaty palms, rapid eye movements and this restrictive skirt.*

Lillibet I: *You had better get used to it or learn to control it, for there is no going back, not unless you fancy public humiliation and self-defeat. You know the others can't afford the trip, but they're here with you, in your heart, cheering you on. Just listen to your heart.*

Lillibet II: *Yeah sure. They're probably in the club downtown right now, drinking, dancing, having completely forgotten this is my big night.*

Lillibet I: *That's unfair. And mean.*

Lillibet II: *You're right, but mean is good. It is what I need right now—to go out there and be mean.*

Lillibet II: *Let's do it then. Are you ready, mean girl?*

Lillibet II: *Never been more ready in my life. Watch this ass as it struts out into that ring. Let us do this. Right here, right now.*

This music hall usually played host to dance troupes who were neat with their belongings and naïve with their relationships. Wrestlers take up more space; their muscles bulkier, their costumes differed from the precise uniformity of the dancers. Theirs were all sparkle and lurex, the caped outfit of the typical superhero. And their egos were less controlled; they had to be larger than life for their audiences, as huge as this performative carnival. From the moment each wrestler arrived backstage to don their costumes, flex the muscles of their alter egos, they practiced, unselfconsciously: their large grins, eyebrows raised like suspension bridges, the forlorn look of a child denied a lollipop. It all took up space.

And there was no space for the twins. Their relationship with the rest of the troupe was based on ambivalence: the men unable to relate to them as peers, rather they were madly jocular in their interactions. Punching their shoulders with huge hands shaped into loose fists, they rubbed the tops of each of the twins' heads as they walked past, as if a magical spirit might arise. Sometimes the twins found themselves lifted from the ground and swung in the outstretched arms of a mountainous wrestler, 'high, high to the sky… fly little one, fly.'

The biggest humiliation, however, was enacted through the allocation of dressing room space: the men of the troupe claimed there was insufficient space for Emilio and Emiliano in their dressing room. Silver Bullet needed space to warm up and stretch his hefty limbs via a sequence of standing lunges; Fishman and Galaxy liked to lavishly apply oils to ensure their biceps glistened in a wondrous way under the spotlights; the Skeleton flung his lanky arms around as he wriggled into his skin-tight bodysuit. In short, their psychological preparation was more akin to an octopus about to mate than a meditation of Sufis preparing to dance. They had no wish for the high-spirited jumpiness of the twins, especially for Emiliano and his constant chatter. The unspoken truth was that they, like others, subconsciously assumed the twins to be minors, with a sexual naivety that needed protecting from the world of bawdy men. They did not want to limit their lascivious talk of whores and liquor, like uncles gathering in a corner at a wedding to leer over the bridesmaids: part of their wrestling preparations were to allow machismo free reign and to park the family man, brother, or dutiful son in a black box firmly outside the door.

All of this led to the twins being allocated a dusty corner of the women's changing room. Here they were largely ignored and occasionally fondly petted. Emilio found this hugely embarrassing; he hated getting changed in the presence of the women wrestlers. He felt self-conscious of his hirsute body but also wanted the women to notice how this same hair now hung in a clump in his armpits and trod a tangled path down his body. Conversely, Emiliano felt that he had hit the jackpot—it was his chance to linger lewd eyes on the contours of women's bodies. He loved watching them squeeze their breasts into tight leotards and openly watched as they bent and twisted in their thongs, naked breasts swinging uninhibited and tight-arsed glutes all around him like desert dunes around a barely hidden oasis. He was in heaven.

Here, unceremoniously, in a dimly lit changing room, with foot-scuffed skirting boards and windows painted shut long ago by a lazy decorator, was where Lillibet first met Emilio and Emiliano. The crowded room was not what she had expected. It certainly was not what she had hoped for. Maybe it was the influence of Hollywood that had long penetrated the collective psyche, but somehow she expected a designated changing room, her name on the door and at least a halo of light bulbs around a bevelled mirror. But this dive was more akin to the changing room of a municipal swimming baths—a no-man's-land, unowned and uncared for. Except it was not a no-man's-land. In the corner were two small men, one of them with his nose in a book and the other scanning the room, either trying to catch the eye of someone, or to catch an eyeful, it was difficult to tell. Either way, what were they doing here? She had seen minis on TV broadcasts of wrestling matches, but her life path had never crossed with such diminutive humans. And now, not only was there a lot of flesh on view in their tiny shorts, but there were two of them! Two the same!

'What are they doing here?' she asked the voluptuous woman changing beside her into an outfit resembling a mermaid with nacreous turquoise scales. 'The two little men. Why are they in here?' Was she the only one who could see them, she wondered? All the others seemed oblivious.

'Oh, they are the Conquestas,' said her new friend, as if this was a viable explanation. Lillibet, understanding she was the new girl in town and not wanting to rock boats, was nonetheless perplexed. She pushed on: 'Why are they in the women's changing rooms?'

'Because there is no space for them in the men's,' replied the mermaid, sharply meeting Lillibet's stare.

'Is it usual to have men changing with the women?' Lillibet continued, unflinching.

'They are not men,' came the reply, as she smudged a sparkle of blue eyeshadow over her left eyelid with a long, elegant but slightly grubby finger. 'They are minis.'

Lillibet was a young woman shaping herself and being shaped by the world. She was beginning to learn the social art of when to speak and when to button up. She was discovering the harsh truth that not everyone was as tolerant of her ways as Consuelo: such acceptance was the domain of a mother. *Best shut up, keep schtum*, she told herself. This containment endured for a good five or six minutes before she decided that the best way to make sense of this strange situation would be to acquaint herself directly with the twins. Ensuring that her costume was all pulled together in the right places, with no flashes of flesh protruding inappropriately, she walked over to their corner.

'Hello. I am Lillibet. Probably the finest cholita wrestler you have ever met.'

Emiliano flashed her a charming, wide-mouthed smile displaying crooked teeth too large for his mouth, whilst Emilio reached out his hand to shake hers. A typical run-of-the-mill introduction between three run-of-the-mill people.

*

Lillibet began to learn about the limits of a body she had assumed boundaryless in strength and stamina. And about connectedness. And humility. But this is too much to dissect in one go—let's take them gradually through this tale and see if we can help her unpack this flurry of experiences, examine it all with fresh eyes and then tinker with, refold, and eventually repack it to face the world again. To reassemble it all neatly and perfectly functioning may take some time, but let's see what we can do for her. Let's try our best. Lillibet deserves our best.

She was magnificent in the ring that evening: just *fab-u-lous*. Her opponent, Scarlett Fox, barely figured in the match: she too wore a tiered petticoat under a green satin skirt, her hair scraped back, her face masked in a dark, heavy foundation which didn't so much slip during the fight, but dissolved below rivulets of sweat commencing at her hairline and dripping as gravity pulled them southwards over her temples and ruddy cheeks, before finally falling in droplets off the edge of her broad, clenched chin.

The bout pushed Lillibet to her limits and beyond. Miguel's training had increased her stamina and strength to a degree capable of facing the strongest of cholitas in the ring, but there was always a payback. In the following days she had to contend with physical and emotional exhaustion. Behind the show woman was a very real person with a developing body, possessing the accompanying human frailties. If she were going to continue on her trajectory of success, she would need a lot more support than, at the outset in her naivety, she had assumed.

When Lillibet entered the ring that evening it was as if the universe had briefly frozen: human movements went into a slow freefall, as if soundwaves passed through deep, thick water. Or at least this was how it felt to Emilio. He shook his head like a puppy after its first submergence in water, flicking off the sensation of curious unfamiliarity. He wanted to dislodge this freeze frame, to resuscitate normality. But simultaneously to savour the delicious warm glow as if nothing mattered apart from the present moment. And Lillibet. He was captivated, captured.

Stepping into that ring, this figure of wonder separated the dancing dust motes and made them swirl around her. She was the centre of the wrestlers' attention. Yet it was more, much more. She was somehow the centre of his senses—his sight, his hearing, all wrapped around her; he even believed he could smell the sweetness of the sweat breaking on her forehead. And how he longed to touch and caress her cheek and feel the vulnerability he could sense she hid behind the caricature. 'It's okay,' he longed to say, 'I'm here now. You can relax. Let go. You are safe to be who you really are. No harm will come to you.' He wanted her to share this sense of home coming, as an unsettled calm emanated from his gut. He hadn't arrived in Maria's aromatic kitchen nor his childhood bedroom with the turquoise washed wall: he had returned to himself, to where he finally felt he could rest and belong.

Lillibet owned the ring; her eyes danced with the spark of fired charcoal, her deep black pupils surrounded by iridescent flashes of red like the filaments of fireflies. Emilio scanned the room and took in one large mass of people who she could bend in time to her rhythmic sway. As she turned on her heel to face him, he saw a light surrounding her torso; it glowed both orange and lavender. Maria had raised him to believe in astrology and frequently invited into their home Romina, a humble woman who roamed from village to village giving readings and drawing charts of planetary constellations, predicting the destinies of her disciples as defined by the arrangement of the stars. Yet she had never allowed this seer to do a reading for her boys. Now, looking back with the renewed perspective of a man, Emilio wondered if this were really the case or if his mother had been protecting him from knowledge she'd discovered during a private reading—were there ominous findings which she had sheltered him from? Perhaps Maria's maternal shield extended to keep from him dark knowledge of his own destiny.

While local villagers came to consult Romina for wisdom concerning their imminent decisions, about which crops to sow under the next full moon, where to best invest carefully accumulated but meagre savings, whether daughters should be married into the neighbour's family, something greater was being withheld from the twins. And, as their debut into the world was only separated by minutes, the stars were aligned in ways that bound their fates as tightly as the fingers of a clenched fist.

Despite all this, Maria dismissed the belief in the supernatural others held tight. She forbade the tarot from her house, arguing that to draw the cards was to meddle with fate. When the spring fayre arrived each Maytime, that unruly caravan of troubadours, storytellers, and acrobats, she refused to visit the palmist, saying that any lines on her hands had been created by the endless scrubbing of floors and the wringing of sheets through her mangle, and the only story they told was that of relentless domestic chores. She was a woman who firmly refused to evoke or dance with any spirits—why would she when she had enough of a challenge forming a dialogue with her own God, to begin to understand what lessons He was sending with the lot He had cast for her?

Having been schooled in his mother's scepticism, Emilio was disorientated by the dancing, vibrating colours he saw around Lillibet's body. His eyes fixed not only on her, but the air around her, and as she moved the colour moved as if intertwined with her being. So captivating, so awe-inspiring. His breathing became slow, calm—each exhale longer than each inhale.

This trancelike state was jolted with the suddenness of a hypnotist snapping his fingers, not with a sharp sound but by the overpowering sense he was being watched.

Watched intently. His eyes shifted focus to bring the scene behind Lillibet into sharp definition, and there he saw Miguel, his deep brown eyes penetrating Emilio's hidden thoughts with a knowing gaze.

Miguel knew what it was like to be a man entrapped by desire, desire leading to a need to possess another, to possess a woman. His jealousy of other men had been his past downfall on more than one occasion when he'd been overtaken by an excruciating combination of his attraction to strong independent women, and his belief that every other man in the vicinity shared this attraction. In the battle between his desires and rational mind, his jealousy had often taken over and fights ensued.

To Miguel, Lillibet and her friends had originally been just a minor irritation, but like a mosquito trapped in the sealed room of a restless sleeper, she had become harder and harder to ignore, and no amount of backhanded swatting would prevent her sucking the lifeblood of his wrestling training out of him. His resistance lasted from February to October until he decided to relent rather than hold it back like a dam, built and maintained by man in a vain attempt to control the power of nature. This flow had led him to grow a curious love for Lillibet; he wasn't in love with her, and his body never stirred at the thought of her, but neither was this a pure paternal love. It was a complex set of emotions driving him to act in ambivalent ways. In training sessions he pushed her not only to the limits of physical strength, but to tears of frustration, yet if hurt in the ring during a bout, he later would tend to her wounds with a carefully prepared compress of comfrey and witch hazel, dabbing at her emerging bruises with the gentleness of a mother tending a fallen infant. He would press her bullied flesh until she had sufficient solace to drop into a peaceful, dreamless sleep.

Now, so far from home, Lillibet embodied many things for Miguel as she stood with her shoulders drawn back, her ballet-slippered feet planted hip-width apart below muscular, toned legs hidden under petticoats. Only a twitch at the base of her clavicle gave away, to close observers, her vulnerability. She was a daughter, a charge he needed to chaperone through this spectacle of folklore, sporting prowess, circus skills and gambling. He knew the wiles of some of the men she was amongst. He knew her claims to independence and capability had been learned in a small town and could easily be crushed like the skeleton of a fledgling bird, if these wolves decided she was their prey. Money was at stake; pride too; reputations. In this setting, Lillibet was a cipher for the ambitions and vanities of men. It was necessary for him to protect her physically from opponents who may want to bend the rules to their advantage in the ring, to barge her with too much force, throw her to the chalk dusted floor with a thrust that could incapacitate her beyond the referee's reverse countdown—ten, nine, eight, seven, six… He also needed to protect her honour. But was this his responsibility as a coach? he wondered. He was in unchartered territory—his male students never thrust him into such a state of complex thoughts and emotions. In the absence of experience, he had to fall back on instinct. Something rose up within him, an innate sense that while in his protection, no man would exploit Lillibet's virginal innocence, at home or as far away as they now were—she was in foreign territory in more than just a geographical sense.

Emilio felt as if a stone had been thrown into the lake in which he had bathed the whole of his life. Hitherto unaware of the stillness of his watery environment, but now ripples emanated from this stone and in turn expanded, to shift the water in ever-increasing shocks. He could feel warning eyes upon him but warning him of what he wasn't sure. Miguel's stare burned into his skull and added to his cocktail of confusion: *why is the coach so angry with me, when all I've done is admire this beautiful creature from afar? What have a done to hurt him, anger him so much? I don't get it.*

Two men locked into any form of combat over a woman, even if only a war of looks, tend to have insufficient bandwidth to realise that a triangle is in play. A third person who is reading the vibrations in the air between the men can from a position of observation, plan a strategy, scope the weft and weave of the tapestry, before the men have realised the desire to thread a needle. The third person is usually a woman who can pass unobserved in plain sight. Pilar, having held back the velvet curtain separating the magic of the main auditorium from the mundanity of the changing rooms, cheered Lillibet as she made her entrance like a homecoming queen. Pilar, as became her role, lingered in the shadows where she could notice without being noticed. And what did she notice? First, she saw Miguel fixing his stare beyond Lillibet's form as she strutted her way round the ring. His sight was focused elsewhere, locked onto one of the minis, the one in the turquoise shorts, the one with the disfigured hand. As if picking apart the strings of a cat's cradle, she then followed the Little Man's line of vision straight back to Lillibet. A perfect invisible triangle had been created between them. And what she saw in the mini's look was not a male desire and lust which Miguel was projecting upon him, but love: a pure and adoring love. His eyes were beatific, glazed with a soft film; his pallor shot through with a blush that rose from his heart chakra, travelling his visage until it appeared to expand beyond the confines of his body and emanate a glow around the top of his forehead. The Little Man had, out of the blue, become lovestruck by her own lovely Lillibet.

Pilar had always known one day she would have to share her friend, that the platonic love of a woman would be overridden by the passion of a man, but never, in her wildest imagination, had she imagined this role to be occupied by a diminutive, muscular man in shiny shorts!

*

As teenagers, Pilar, Lillibet and Eva had spent many evenings lounging in one of their parents' yards. They would be tired from the sultry heat of the early day, and the sense-making of the adult world they were entering, tired from the surge of adolescent hormones running through their blood, from adjusting to the loss of blood from their bodies each month. These evenings centred around the exchange of confidences, fantasies, dreams: sometimes about their careers, sometimes about the houses they would design and furnish with textures of velvet and damask, and sometimes their future lovers, husbands or unborn children. The men they fantasised about were largely montages from the images of sportsmen and film stars from glossy magazines. They constructed men as composite figures of desired characteristics, like compiling a criminal photofit. These men's eye colour and depth (always a brooding brown), height (tall but muscular and broad, never tall and thin), hair (thick with curls, inviting fingers to sink into it), and clothes (stylish, well-ironed, fashionable but not too much so, and slightly ruffled to convey a lack of fastidiousness and devil-may-care) passed through their minds. They were yet to learn that life is not a work of romantic fiction. That life wasn't always lived by a set of binary opposites. Life was going to throw them curveballs in many ways, particularly in terms of the soulmates for whom they would open their hearts.

*

Pilar rolled her shoulders back and took a deep breath. 'This is not what I think,' she muttered to herself. *I am reading this wrong. Honestly, sometimes my imagination needs to be brought under control.* There was no risk here, she decided. It would not be necessary to adjust her image of double dating, herself and Lillibet seated in restaurants of deep-coloured sumptuous fabrics and stainless steel with solicitous waiters, men seated opposite who would make every other woman and gay man at adjacent tables green with envy. Just because this tiny wrestler had been struck by a thunderbolt it wouldn't be reciprocated by her friend. There, before her, was her lovely Lillibet, resplendent in her meticulously selected outfit, holding the space, the attention of every man, and many of the women in the room captured. Inevitably, she of such charisma wouldn't give so much as the time of day to this small man—he was punching way above his weight—literally.

*

Emilio and Emiliano met their shadow opposite in Maria's womb. Or was it merely an encounter with another part of themselves? An egg divided into two surely at a psychological level remains part of the same whole. But the perceived rush for the birth channel imposed competition in them from their beginning in this world. 'Yes, you are identical twins, but which one of you is the eldest? Which came out first?' And this was just the beginning—the questions by impudent strangers kept flowing, layer upon layer of who is that and who is the other. Who is the strongest? The weakest? The clever one? The sporty one? Who is the sensitive one? Who is the tallest, the handsomest, the artist, the scholar, the good son, the most passionate lover, the kind neighbour, the wealthiest, the healthiest? And on and on and on— resistance by either twin to the tide of comparative categorisation was futile—it just took too much energy. And so they succumbed and adopted their roles, each in comparison to the other. Each became the other's shadow.

*

It was after the spectacular and gratifying evening's show when Red Fox burst through without a rapped knuckle on a wooden door, into the ladies' dressing room, and shouted above the cacophony of gleeful chitter chatter across to the twins: 'So which one of you boys is the party goer?'

With a glint of mischief in his eye, Emiliano announced: 'Me of course! Always!'

'Then get dressed quickly buddy, there are fans and whores in this town who require our attention,' shouted the lord of misrule. Flashing a gold-toothed smile. 'Stage door in ten minutes—the real show is about to hit town.'

As Emilio sat in front of the dressing mirror, its glaze long ago worn thin to a sepia tarnish, his brother assiduously averted his gaze. To meet his eye would have exposed him to far too many probing questions, all unspoken, but within the supercharged energy currents firing between them.

Emilio slapped dollops of unctuous cold cream onto his cheeks and used it to soothe his skin left red and blotchy by the wrestling mask rubbing against his sweating face. The rawness of his complexion resembled the aftermath of a teenager's prolonged crying fit at the injustices of the world. His brother meanwhile hurried with staccato movements, pulling his trousers over his wrestling shorts, his unbuttoned shirt over his head. He hopped from foot to foot to put on his trainers without the inconvenience of unknotting the laces. He had the unbridled eagerness of a puppy promised a walk in the woods, anxious that his humans might depart the house without him.

Emilio didn't mind the prospect of a quiet evening. He could tidy their corner of the dressing room, making sure their costumes were ready for tomorrow's show and then pick up a tortilla from the café across the road and eat it whilst reading the final chapter of the murder mystery novel he was enjoying. In peace. An introvert's perfect evening. Yet other thoughts pervaded his mind: *why have I been excluded from this invitation? Am I somehow lacking something? Why don't they find me entertaining enough to be included? Don't they even like me? Did I do something, say something wrong?* He folded his shorts, then his brother's shorts while the ambivalent desire to escape his solitude, to be part of the motley crew of firecrackers, tumbling out of the stage door with the flamboyance of a self-conscious carnival taunted his quiet mind. He rubbed at the brittle quick of his cuticles, inflicting just enough pain to keep the threat of tears at bay, knowing the crowd of revellers would not even give him a second thought as their evening seamlessly unfolded into night-time. He would be forgotten by them, but maybe not by Lillibet.

*

'Tequila shots all round please barman,' proclaimed Red Fox as he slapped his octopus-sized hand on the beer-soaked bar. 'Let the merriment begin.' The troupe demanded attention through their exuberance, each still driven by the heightened adrenaline of the wrestling match, unable to relinquish the sheer pleasure of being feted by a captivated audience. The group moved en masse with soft, undefined edges, swaying with dynamic energy. Emiliano always made sure he was close to the centre of this dance, using his ability to duck through his compatriots' legs to his advantage and slide his way through gaps in the organism. Heat emanated from the toned muscular bodies of his friends; Emiliano treasured the sensation of sharing garlic-infused sweat, of pushing his body against the warmth of others who would meet his pressure with their own, the laws of physics keeping them in fluid but constant balance. He filled his lungs with warm, putrid air as if it were nectar from the gods, greedily inhaling the oxygen exhaled by the others. He knew he was where he wanted to be. He belonged. He had come home.

Shot after shot of burning liquor was downed by the group, sliding down their throats like lava on the sides of an erupting volcano. Strangers in the bar made public displays of standing them a round as coins were slapped on the bar time after time. 'Fill them up again barman. Right to the top. Don't be stingy with our visitors—let's show them what a generous town we are.' And in turn the wrestlers performed for their drinks: they slapped each other's backs, shook hands like disingenuous politicians, and posed for photos to be uploaded to social media within seconds. 'Look at me. With him, I am the epicentre of everything. Look. At. Me.'

The wrestlers' identities were always protected by the disguise of their masks—hidden behind the vibrant satin like a bride's veil concealing her demure virginity. A local man, unsteady on his tequila-infused legs, approached Colossus, putting an arm around his shoulders, invading his body space with a drunken overconfidence and a reeking sweat from his armpits. With bloodshot eyes, he drew Colossus to look straight at him. 'Take the mask off mate. Let's see your face. We're your friends after all,' he slurred. 'Always will be. That mask must be hot. Take it off—c'mon mate.' A hint of impatience slid into his tone, betraying his false bravado. Colossus, trained in self-control, didn't blink, didn't speak, barely flinched, using his steady eyes alone to keep the drunk in his place.

'Come away, Carlos.' His marginally more sober friend stepped in, unwound his friend's arm from the wrestler's shoulder, realigned the lost balance this movement generated, and escorted him tenderly like a fawn on its spindly legs protected by its mother. Guiding him back to their table and although trying to settle his friend quietly in place with the gentle care of men who have travelled life's precarious path since school days, the drunk moved his body down towards his stool, misjudged its edge and hit the floor with a heavy thud. An ironic victory cheer went up from the corner of the room, closely followed by the irregular tempo of mismatched applause. The drunk lay immobile and confused: was he the source of humour? He closed his eyes, a dribble of spit running down his chin: 'You can all go to hell, the lot of you.'

The main action, however, took place towards the centre of the room. A space had been cleared, stools and small round tables pushed aside with the force of a centrifuge, the desire for competition between the wrestlers had still not abated. Taking turns they attempted to pick up a meticulously placed match box shell with each of their bulbous noses, protuberances clearly not evolved for this challenge. The competitors knelt as if in prayer, hands behind their backs. A circle of spectators formed, urging them on. Lillibet, having slipped into the bar half an hour behind the others, kept a dignified distance; she perched on a bar stool, interspersing each shot of tequila with a glass of water. Despite being young, her female instinct had crept in, warning her not to lose control. She always knew that she must be able to get herself back to her caravan unaided. She scanned the room for Miguel but could find no sign of him. Smoothing her skirt over her knees she avoided meeting the eyes of any of the strangers in the bar. *Drop your shoulders, they are riding up. Your neck is short, it's not flattering*, she told herself. *They are liquid. Imagine they are liquid, not stone.*

Emiliano rubbed his sweat-drenched palms down the course, worn corduroy of his trousers and stepped forward: he imagined himself on a stage heralded by a singular spotlight, trained on him alone. He tasted expectation in the stale air of the room—sweet and bitter. A mixture of the tequila and the tiredness that follows an action-packed match, coupled with his supreme effort in watching Lillibet while not being seen to do so, all combined to constrict his vision into a tight, dark tunnel. Everything beyond this line of vision swam in a soft pulsing sea. An electric tingle ran up and down his spine—he had been invited to join in the game. He had been included; he was one of the boys. For the first time he was the centre of their boisterous action, no longer on the periphery. Away from his brother he could be normal, not one half of a human freak show. While assuming his position on his knees, ready to prove himself a good sport, he cast his eyes up at the figure sitting at the bar. He knew this moment of pleasure would be sealed if he found Lillibet observing him with admiration, recognising him as a man surrounded by friends, joining in with the sport of men. He wanted them to exchange a fleeting look, locking them, in a moment, into an unspoken union of mutual understanding. It would be a beginning—a footprint in the sand—a promise.

'Do it. Do it.'

The chanting of the circle gained a tribal momentum. Tables were rhythmically banged with empty, hollow sounding beer glasses.

'Do it. Do it.'

The noise of the crowd morphed from a chorus into a bray. There was a phantom taste of blood being spilt. Emiliano felt the unfamiliar texture of satin on his chapped hands as his wrists were bound behind his back. A matchbox was flamboyantly placed on the footprint-infested floor, in the centre of the invisible circle before him. Again he stole a quick glance up at the bar: Lillibet was deep in conversation with a local ruddy-skinned woman. Their bodies mirrored each other as they leant forwards, laughing and touching each other's wrists in a female bond of intimacy alien to him.

This was not the scenario Emiliano had written for himself—it was not supposed to play out like this. The evening he had scripted as the climax to his glory—he played the part of the leading man with Lillibet cast as his leading lady. They would be a glorious couple of beauties emanating a hypnotic energy. A tightening band of tension took hold across his forehead as he realised he found himself in the chorus. Always in the chorus.

The chanting crowd was getting louder and louder. They wanted action. They wanted to be entertained. Glasses were banged, feet stamped. Emiliano took a deep breath, pointed his nose towards the matchbox, eager now to get this undignified charade over with. Speed is the enemy of preparedness: Emiliano's internal imbalance rippled from his head through his body and he found himself toppling forwards, nose first onto the filthy floor, his hands still tied behind his back, unable to break his fall. His forehead reverberated with a bang as he fell on the floorboards—bone against wood, and in a sea of humiliation rolled in bondage trying to right himself. Among the braying of drunken men who had lured their prey into a cruel trap, for their own entertainment the only image Emiliano had in his mind was of his brother sitting alone at home on the sofa in their caravan lit by the gentle glow of a side lamp—calm, quiet, poised. He felt a deep longing to hug and be hugged by his brother—to be locked in that amniotic embrace of just the two of them, when they were once together, safe from this harsh world.

*

The rap at the caravan door was more brittle than Pilar anticipated. Everyone in the troupe knew Lillibet enjoyed, or more precisely needed, her lengthy daily siesta and that to interrupt this was like stirring the wrath of a python.

Anticipating a repeat of the rap, a knuckle ready to rattle the metal door again, she leapt forward and flung the door wide, assisted by a gush of wind gathering in the acacia trees, preparing to swirl and dance. Pilar had previously agreed to an afternoon stroll with Heli, the calmest of the mariachi singers. For weeks she had resisted this woman's attempts to forge a friendship—the proffered cups of nettle tea, the rub between her shoulder blades easing the tension as they watched the compelling spectacle of Lillibet dominating yet another opponent in the ring, the invitation to join a card game with the other mariachis. Pilar told herself Lillibet was enough—enough to consume her whole focus, to care for her both domestically and psychologically. Lillibet was rapidly, day by day, becoming more of what her own mother would call 'a handful', and Pilar was expediently trying to expand the reach of her hands and heart to keep her friend held and anchored. Endlessly she tried to counter the whirlwind of attention and flattery drawing Lillibet in from all quarters: some Lucha Libre fans would trail in the wake of the troupe from town to town, buying prime seats for every match, forming a reliable circle of adoration. To the media Lillibet was a darling—bright, young, vivacious, with an air of mystery. She made good copy. Such a relentless spotlight was taking its toll, however. Some days Pilar felt as if she herself was turning to vapour. She no longer felt a firm footing on the ground beneath her. Days blurred and the more well-defined and vibrant Lillibet became, the less visible Pilar felt. As if they were a total sum in equilibrium and when one gained, the other lost. Surely if one grew, the other should also, by association? She had a throbbing dread, located in her solar plexus, of anyone asking her: 'So tell me about yourself Pilar. What are your passions and fears?' For it felt like there was nothing to tell. She could only define herself in relation to Lillibet.

When Heli passed her a note on Tuesday at supper suggesting a stroll the following afternoon, she had felt the delicate opportunity opening, a way to test whether a mild agoraphobia was seeping into her marrow. Could she engage with a world beyond their caravan and the wrestling arena, she wondered? Where was the danger? After all, it was merely an invitation to a stroll, and surely 'stroll' is one of the most innocuous words? What possible harm could come? Nothing so time limited as a stroll could disturb the bond she had with Lillibet, surely?

Yet, when she flung open the caravan door to reprimand Heli for her pervasive knocking, Pilar was surprised to find the Skeleton precariously balancing on the rock their substitute doorstep. She was even more surprised to find him waving a rainbow kite at her, and behind that prism of refracted light, a broad grin filled with perfectly aligned teeth. The Skeleton never smiled when in character. It would ruin his image, be fundamentally wrong for this symbol of bodily fragility and death to be chirpy. But now here he was grinning. On her doorstep. Waving around a kite!

The Skeleton wasn't dressed in his wrestler's costume. In the ring he cut a striking figure in his tight black lycra bodysuit, painted with the bones of a human man both on his back and torso. Unlike the other wrestlers with their garish satin masks, his was a black hood with a white painted skull and holes for his eyes, nostrils and mouth allowing him to see, snort and sigh. When the lights of each auditorium dimmed, the audience could no longer see his human shape. Instead, the vision before them was his jangly spine and ribs which he beat with a luminous stick to the rhythm of a familiar children's nursery rhyme—destined to haunt their bedtimes for weeks to come.

His movements were always staccato, creating the impression of bones clashing in the absence of the body's shock absorbers, muscle and sinew. This was not a body at rest—it was a body seeking answers to the question of death, answers which lay beyond each human lifespan. He was *memento mori* in motion. Children were terrified as he jangled around like a marionette, appearing as if his movements were controlled by an invisible force wanting to humiliate him by percussively shaking his bones against each other.

This caricature didn't scare Pilar, partly because she knew he was like the whole troupe, merely a human in costume, and partly because she was too logical to believe his skeletal, deathly qualities would remain embodied in the man once his costume was removed. Once the mask came off there remained flesh and blood. But mostly her overriding emotion towards him was indifference; to her he was one of a melee, one more extroverted performer constituting the mere backdrop to the rising star and electric energy of Lillibet. They played in the shadows while her friend danced in the light.

Prior to his knocking, Pilar had been distracted by the caravan sink. She had almost finished unblocking it from another bout of expanding couscous. In her domestic idleness, Lillibet perpetually cleared her dinner plate down the sink rather than using the bin. Consuelo would be horrified if she were to witness her daughter's domestic laziness. The sink had become an endless source of frustration to Pilar as she inevitably ended up with the task of unblocking the U-bend. Today, plunger in hand, and with rubber gloves sprayed with food debris, she found herself wondering what her life would be like now had she devoted more time to educating and developing herself—what would her true character be. She longed to be reading philosophy and poetry, even theology. She longed to be exploring the higher aspects of the human condition. Willing this task to become a meditation, she contemplated the relevance of the swelling couscous trapped in the drainage system. What was this to the cosmos? Did it represent a need for matter to expand until it reached an externally fabricated limit? Or had Lillibet's repeated creation of these blockages been sent as a challenge, to teach her patience and to stop, as the westerners were so fond of saying, sweating the small stuff?

Either way, it was a concern that arose weekly with horrid predictability. And as her mind addressed these thoughts yet again like a clock's mechanisms turning cogs repeatedly, the Skeleton rapped his bony knuckles on the flimsy caravan door.

'Greetings lady,' he announced with exaggerated flamboyance that barely camouflaged his nervousness. 'Would you care to join me on this fine afternoon and set flight this precious object?' He circled the kite around the top of his head dancing it into a figure of eight, a symbol of infinity.

At times of confusion our minds focus-in on small details and spot any incongruity, trying to seek certainty in an uncertain world. Pride will be taken in finding the chink which highlights imperfection—the crack where light gets in. We save ourselves from chaos on a universal scale by narrowing our vision. As did Pilar in this muddle.

'But the air is still today, there's no wind to lift the kite.'

'A mere detail madam. I can command the wind. I can draw back the oceans and realign the stars for you.' He flourished the damned kite again but this time the red string became knotted around his scrawny wrist, and in his attempt to push it off it ravelled further.

'Why are you talking like that?' she asked, squinting at him through the sunlight seeping through the caravan portal.

'I thought you might like to be entertained.'

'Why would you think that?' she retorted, regretting sounding so harsh.

'Okay,' he sighed. "I would like to spend time with you. Just with you. I want to get to know you. You interest me, and you're beautiful. But you're always with Lillibet—never alone. I thought at siesta time I might get you alone. I thought you might enjoy company. My company!' Once he began, the Skeleton, like many unused to verbalising their emotions, didn't know how to stop. 'I thought you would enjoy playing with the kite. With me. Me, you, and the kite. We could try to fly it on the beach, even without the wind. I'm sure it will still go high, higher than the treetops.'

'Shh.' She brought her index finger to her lips. His awkwardness was endearing, but only to a point. 'Even if I wanted to, I can't because Heli is coming to call for me so that we can take a walk together.'

He cast his eyes down. 'No she's not. I'm making a mess of this aren't I?"

The scene he had planned, the script he had written for this encounter in which Pilar joyfully grabbed her sunhat and sandals and ran gaily with him, giggling as he took her hand, the pair of them stumbling over the dunes towards the beach: it wasn't exactly going to plan.

'But Heli was going to call for me at 2 o'clock, and it's now a quarter past. I'm not sure where she is. It's not like her to be late.' Pilar tapped her watch to check it's functioning. She really wasn't getting it!

'I asked her not to come,' confessed the now subdued Skeleton. 'I asked her so I could come in her place. I thought you might have said no if I'd asked you directly.'

Pilar was unfamiliar with male attention. She was certainly unused to being courted. Up until now she had lived so much of her life in Lillibet's shadow, she had almost become invisible—or so she assumed. Consequently, she was unsure what was proper and where lines of convention were drawn. Even so, she felt an invisible line had been crossed. The metal of the caravan reflecting the heat of the afternoon felt headache-inducing. There were two alternatives and the need to make a quick decision: alternative one was to retreat to the stagnant air of the caravan and continue unblocking the sink; alternative two was to give in to the invitation from this gangly, jangly man and maybe, just maybe, have fun. She lifted a few strands of wayward hair sticking to the back of her neck in the heat, and to disguise a slight flush of eagerness she felt rising in her chest, turned her back on him and re-entered the curtained dark of the caravan.

'Okay. But you're going to need to untangle that string while I find my sandals.'

*

'Pilar,' mumbled Lillibet. 'Pilar, can you bring me tea please? I'm awake. I'm awake Pilar,' she called, with the cotton wool muffle of a barely completed siesta.

She rolled over, picked up her faithful, much-travelled alarm clock and noted it was 4.40. She must have been asleep ages, a good half-hour extra than usual. The sun still penetrated the flimsy cotton curtains. She felt the air outside move—the post-siesta world stirring faster than she was. Her competitive temperament made her hate the prickly sensation of being behind in anything.

Kicking aside her tangled, sticky bedsheet, she called out more irritably: 'Pilar, where are you? Why didn't you wake me at 4?'

No reply.

Pulling a t-shirt over her camisole, Lillibet took the

four steps from her bedroom to the galley kitchen. Empty. She checked Pilar's bedroom. Empty. The only unexplored room was the postage stamp-sized loo. Empty. For the first time since they'd embarked on the road together, Pilar wasn't there, ready and eager to tend to her friend's needs.

Lillibet tousled her hair into a rough ponytail, wayward strands refusing to be constrained, and hoiked her t-shirt off again. All the caravan windows and doors were closed, trapping stale and stagnant air. Nothing was moving. She tapped her fingernails on the formica dining room table, *where is she, where on earth is she?* and then flung the door open with such force it hit the rubber stopper and rebounded. Every action induces a reaction, and the caravan reacted with a shudder of disapproval. Mateo, the impossibly handsome moustached newest member of the troupe, was wandering past looking dapper in linen trousers and a starched white shirt with sharply ironed lines running down each arm. He paused mid-stride, and visibly raised an arched eyebrow at the violence of Lillibet's exit from her caravan.

'All okay Lillibet?'

'Fine,' she retorted, regretting her obvious irritability.

He shrugged and continued on his way, smugly appreciative of his own inner calmness.

Lillibet plonked her backside on the stone step, worn smooth through years of loyal service supporting feet descending and ascending caravans on this site, witnessing the unblemished soles of children enjoying first holidays, middle-aged careworn women carrying baskets of washing scrubbed by hand to hang to dry crisp in the heat of the day, and men who had drunkenly staggered to their beds late, some amorous towards their wives, others spoiling for a fight. But the stone had never witnessed a bottom plonked with such despondency as Lillibet's this day. She was highly trained and primed to respond to anything or anyone who crossed her path, so finding herself devoid of an external stimulus she was at a loss—the world came to her. However, once she had calmed herself just a little and allowed this stimulus vacuum space to breathe, her senses expanded by the second and she listened. Really listened. First, she heard birds rousing for their dusk chorus not yet having taken flight into the still air. This was intermingled with the dry bray of a donkey as if he was in conversation with a rooster, each taking turns to call and respond in a verbal tennis match. Sound carries in waves, but it also carries in layers, and the more closely Lillibet listened, the more of these layers she could decipher. She heard the high-pitched laugh of a woman dancing through the air as if in harmony with the animal world. The emotion evoked by this tinkling laugh rose from Lillibet's heart centre, and before her brain could formulate awareness of how little joy there currently was in her life and yearn for it, the feeling became embodied and rose from her chest to her throat in a choking, stifled cry. Lillibet's well-developed barbed wire forces of defence had only been relaxed a few minutes and a rush of longing and loneliness had surged through like a juggernaut down a deserted road on a dark and starless night.

The laughter tinkled again, this time louder—more rounded, more confident. Just as Lillibet was expelling a breath full of regret, she recognised the pitch of that laugh. *It's Pilar. That's Pilar's giggle.* She's nearby, somewhere behind the trees. And she's having fun! *But where? Exactly? Doing what?* Lillibet realised she hadn't heard that laugh for a long time; possibly the last time was before they embarked on this unending wrestling tour. That laugh had been the soundtrack to their girlhood when Pilar's large heart had found joy in every circumstance and encouraged Lillibet to relax her seriousness and laugh with her. *When did we both stop laughing?*

Lillibet stood on tiptoe, directing her gaze towards where the joyous sound was emanating. Their caravan braced its spine against the ombre dunes, the salt wash leaving a patina of silver and green kaleidoscopic fragments on the shell. Beyond the dunes she could see two figures, recognisable figures: that curve of the hip, that lanky awkwardness with sharp bodily edges that contrasted with the rolling waves and undulating dunes. Set against the soft colours of the landscape was a kite, an orange and purple kite echoing the hues of the sunset bleeding its way down to the horizon.

The kite and the people danced in unison; this wasn't the struggle of the wrestling ring where muscles and wiles were pitted each against the other until one side surrendered. Rather, this was a marriage of movement between two people and their environment.

Lillibet sat back down rather too heavily than she intended. A jolt to her coccyx jarred up the length of her spine. There was a sensation in her chest she couldn't immediately identify. It was heavy, awkward. Later she came to recognise this as an insidious cocktail of envy and unbearable loneliness.

*

Pilar couldn't pinpoint when the regular sound of Gabriel tapping on the caravan door during siesta time shifted from a rap of bony knuckles on a coffin lid to evoking the first piano chords of a symphony. For now, her Skeleton had become known as Gabriel, his actual name. He was a person, a man, rather than a character temporarily out of his costume.

Lillibet had taken to implying that an invitation from Pilar and Gabriel to join them on one of their afternoon sojourns would be welcomed. In retort, Pilar had chosen to overlook the subtext of exclusion and firmly told her friend her afternoon rest was a crucial part of her training regime. "You mustn't tire yourself out or your performance will suffer. Relax and enjoy the peace and quiet, just kick back."

Knowing she shouldn't resent her loyal friend for these episodes of fun, jealously still seeped into Lillibet's heart, despite having been enjoying the spotlight for so long. She had been the one taking the glory and making a name and money for herself for the last two years. Yet still felt this twinge of envy towards Pilar itched her psyche as a repetitive refrain. Well, refrain was possibly an understatement if she were honest; her feelings if left unchecked were more like a torrent of longing for something she'd never had.

She was bearing witness to a growing bond between the two kite flyers. In consequence, Gabriel was somehow becoming less jagged, and Pilar seemed larger as if she was occupying more than just her physical body, but also filling the air. And she was doing so with a golden glow others were noticing but not quite able to put their fingers on.

'Have you changed your skin cream Pilar?'

'Is Lillibet being less demanding?"

'Have you started a different exercise regime?'

Lillibet felt her role in this blossoming was merely a passive observer: she watched the gaze that passed the two companions during training sessions, at mealtimes, at social events. They were drawn together with a comfortable magnetism.

*

Inevitably, Emilio had also spotted this strengthening connection between Pilar and Gabriel. After all, he spent so much time observing Lillibet it was inevitable he would become drawn into her stories. A pattern was repeated each day of the watched and watchful.

It was an uneven, ragged dynamic. But it was as it was.

Emilio should have stayed in the background, remained as the observer and not entered the fray. If only he hadn't shifted from audience to actor. Things wouldn't then have unfolded into the sequence of events that brought him to collapse in a weeping mess on Maria's maternal bosom on that languid summer's day when the village sundial was shadow-shifting into its last quarter.

*

Like most introverts Emilio's best friends were his books. Stories helped him feel less alone with his thoughts—they were his way of making sense of the world vicariously, living through the eyes of fictionalised events experienced by a range of protagonists. He gravitated mostly to stories of romantic male figures capable of expressions of deeply felt love for inaccessible women. These women represented a range of 'too' for the would-be heroes: too beautiful, too successful, too happily married. Ahead of the romantic men was a quest to be undertaken to win those they so desired. They needed to become 'more': more wealthy, more athletic, more sensitive to win hearts and souls. Emilio could relate to these characters, but there was always a threshold across which their experiences failed to pass beyond for Emilio to feel they were fully resonating, for him to feel that he was not ultimately alone.

Thresholds are occupied by djinns, fairies, and spirits. They were the places that filled Emilio with wonder yet instilled trepidation. His longing to connect with Lillibet was forever growing, and his need to express this was accumulating not only in his heart but his muscles as if a volcanic eruption was rumbling, readying to erupt. If he were to comfortably occupy his body again, he would need to step over the threshold from the fictional worlds of his books into real life, and face whatever tricks the djinns might play on him.

And so this is how the poetry began, the route of romantic expression throughout the ages. From Rumi to Tagore to Byron to Neruda, with many a detour.

After years of childhood struggles even to hold a pencil, let alone write, Emilio conceded defeat in his school studies around the same time his teachers gave up on him. He put his disappointments in a box, sealed tight in the way only a damaged child can. From then he muddled through life's necessities of form-filling and inscribing niceties in birthday cards, until he was able to embrace the wonders of technology and the joyous experience of completing written tasks with his two index fingers, devoid of the hampering restrictions caused by the absence of his right thumb. Nevertheless, any form of writing, in life admin or emotional expression, remained arduous, tedious, and demanding. It wasn't for him.

Neither was talking, really. As an introvert in an extrovert's world, Emilio often felt at odds. Why, he asked himself, had he chosen to place himself in an environment of performers and exhibitionists—somatic artists who though outwardly collaborative, were competing for the attention of any audience member afforded them. Emilio became lost among the clamour. He wanted to turn down the volume of the external world, forever, causing the noise in his head to amplify. Many times he watched with envy at his brother's ease; his confidence begot confidence. Emiliano appeared to consume no energy in fitting in, conversely buoyed by all the fraternising. His brother had finally succeeded in assimilating as one of the boys. In their corner of the dressing room he had blended as one of the girls, shapeshifting with smoothness.

Emilio chose his books not only as a place of solace: they were also his constant companion, much to the impatience of his twin.

'Why are you always curled in that bunk with a pile of books? Why don't you just get down here and mix? You're so antisocial. It's not just me saying this, the others think so too. You'll run out of books to bury your head in—then what will you do, eh?'

Emiliano was in full transmit mode with no interest in turning his dial to 'receive'. In any case, Emilio kept his own counsel and merely responded by turning to his printed page companions.

One unusually damp, humid afternoon on a day of impasse when there would be no evening match along with a rest from training sessions, Emilio, curled like a comma with his book, sensed his yearning to connect with Lillibet becoming unbearable. She was the last of his thoughts before nighttime sleep took him into his dreamscape. She was the first of his thoughts on waking each morning. Frequently she flitted gracefully through his daytime mind in her ballerina slippers, with her bowler hat tilted over her eyes and a teasing smile.

He had taken to reading the love poems of Sabines, which spoke to him. Sabines understood him across the years and countries, almost as if he too had met Lillibet and crafted parallel feelings of love into a collection of beautifully framed words. Emilio never failed to gravitate to the master's sparse yet precision of words that captured this essence of his feelings. Such is the joy of all poetic lovers and lovers of poetry.

Sabines spoke directly to him. There was no interference on the line, no white noise disturbing the connection. They understood love the same way. The words on the page reached out with empathy and tenderness. The master's syntax was a source of wonder.

Emilio sought times to be alone with these poems, as being in a quiet space with Sabines felt akin to being with Lillibet. He could so easily imagine stroking her chin, smoothing her hair, even finding peace by resting his lovestruck head on her warm soft breast. He had taken to copying lines of the poet's in his own spider crawl handwriting. For the first time in his life, writing came to him without the familiar pain in his hand and without the self-consciousness of the final uneven scribble. It was as if he wrote to Lillibet herself, imagining her taking comfort in the words, appreciating the intense beauty of his feelings. Finally, he had found a language and a connection within this ever-spinning world, writing lines about the the foolishness of his love, the dizzy absurdity of feeling he was in a dream when he was walking with her.

To Emilio, the words he held on this paper were calligraphy, beautifully crafted shapes. He longed to carve a future that contained just him, his love, and these words, away from the maelstrom of their lives. The only people with whom he would share this fantasy world would be their beautiful children—two small daughters, merely smaller versions of Lillibet with tiny petticoats and perfectly crafted bowler hats falling from their heads as they danced and tumbled through sunlit gardens.

Ambivalence coursed through his experience of copying Sabines's words, like the sensual pleasure of eating too much delicious but overly-sugared cake. He found joy in imagining that one day his mouth might form these words into a whisper, uttered in a darkened bedroom with Lillibet lying beside him, her eyelids lightly closed to better focus her auditory senses. This scene of sensual beauty was tempered by the impression he had made with these words on the page. His ugly handwriting a scrawl: jagged and uneven. The excess pressure he needed to merely control his pen appeared on the paper as engraved ruts, as if written by a person consumed by anger. His real-life relationship with her was of casual friendship, members of the same troupe bonded by sport.

He detected friendliness, but was it his imagination or a slightly condescending nod to his small stature? Was she yet another person unable to detect the man occupying his small body? Whispering poetry to her, even Sabines's magical lines, wasn't on the cards. Not yet anyway.

If he couldn't speak or whisper, the only option left was that age-old method used by romantic figures throughout the ages—writing to the object of his adoration. A love letter. A billet-doux. A perfumed envelope with a waxen seal. A note inscribed on watermarked paper. Emilio was acutely aware though that in stories these letters are always written in elegant, cursive script with gold-nibbed pens, not sweated onto the page in the frenetic script of a man missing his opposable digit. No, if he were to write to Lillibet it would have to be in another's hand. This is where Alfredo came in, the vihuela player in their mariachi band.

Emilio and Alfredo had formed a friendship over evening games of canasta and chess. Neither were barflies, preferring reflective evenings in solitude or quiet companionship with one another sharing card games. Bonding was easy. They saw nothing wrong (or at least they never expressed disapproval!) with the raucous tequila-fuelled evenings in every bar so enjoyed by the others—it just wasn't for them personally.

During their card games, Alfredo always kept the tally, written in a little moleskine notebook with a marbled indigo blue and golden pen. He kept both items tucked in his top shirt pocket, typical of a man of meticulous and conventional appearance. Most of the troupe adopted a dress style in their downtime which could only be described as somewhere between bohemian and sports casual. For the men this tended to involve baggy, well-worn joggers on their lower bodies contrasting with garish shirts on their torsos. The peacocking flamboyance typical of them in the ring wasn't solely about theatre and spectacle—it was something that ran through their lifeblood as performers. Any chance to display vibrant plumage and attract attention was never passed up. The women were no different: their off-duty fashion reversed that of the men, with bright skirts, long enough to skim the ground, coupled with baggy sports sweatshirts and hoodies.

Alfredo was his own man though. His daywear gave the impression he was heading for a meeting in a tech company, or maybe an English businessman only comfortable when protected by the shell of his work persona. In short, Alfredo wore beige chinos with a razor-sharp crease pressed precisely down the middle and paired with a pale blue short-sleeved shirt. His alter ego in the mariachi band wore topaz turquoise satin trousers and a white shirt with a ruffle evocative of the best meringues, divided horizontally by a handsome cumber band. The pièce de résistance of his outfit a pair of well-polished Cuban heels, boots crafted in the best leather and dyed the matching hue of his trousers.

Being a man with a limited range of expressive emotions, he tended towards a composed demeanour which he would switch back to automatically once the exaggerated expressiveness typical of his band's performance was complete. He was unlike the other guys who sought outlets for their adrenaline and over-pumped hearts, fuelled by the exertion of the physicality of the wrestling along with the excitement of the spectacle.

Alfredo was more likely to be found sipping a herbal tisane, peering over his horn-rimmed glasses and jotting things into his notebook. Or sometimes, absorbed in a game of chess or canasta with whoever would sit quietly with him.

Emilio decided this was the guy to help him woo Lillibet.

Naïvely, he assumed this would involve him confiding his secret love. Why naïve? Because for many this love was blatant. It could be seen in the little man's look of adoration, prone to changing quickly into a stammering blush on the rare but precious moments his love spoke with him. The wrestlers had been trained to read the slightest facial expression or tensing muscle. It was an art essential when predicting opponents' tactics in the ring. Over time, their intuition became more attuned, like the conductor who can sense the lead violinist will miss her cue by the slightest change in her exhalation as she lifts her bow. Their sport was 20 percent physical, 80 percent psychological, so while they might appear an assemblage of overtrained muscle and sinew, hidden from the audience was their tuned skill in person reading. All this meant detecting Emilio's admiration of Lillibet had gone way beyond Miguel's protective observations and rippled throughout the troupe. It was, however, unacknowledged, undiscussed: they may have collectively relished the sport of gossip as much as they did wrestling, but their fondness of 'the little fellas' exempted the twins from being the subject of tittle-tattle mockery.

If Emilio were to share poetry with Lillibet, he would need a scribe, someone who could produce handwriting as elegant as his feelings. It will be no surprise that Alfredo always produced admirably precise handwriting. It was a simple match of demand and supply. One day at dusk, as the shadows dissolved and the light faded over a game of chess, as fireflies displayed their phosphorescent light, flitting between the pieces on the board, Emilio cleared his throat: 'Alfredo.' …a pause… 'I wonder if you could help me one day soon?'

Knight to b4.

'Help you with your moves bud?' replied his opponent.

Rook took knight.

A long contemplative silence ensued, an ambiguous silence—was Emilio contemplating his next chess or conversational move?

Queen to e6.

'With writing. I need help with writing to someone.'

'Is it to the lady with raven plaits and the grace of a hummingbird by any chance?"

Bishop to g5. Checkmate.

With the flick of his wrist Emilio knocked his king down, conceding defeat.

'Yes. To Lillibet. I must communicate my feelings for her. But my own words are inadequate. I want to use Sabines, you know, the great poet Sabines, as my channel.'

From this point a relationship based on quiet respect sprang up between the two men. The following Tuesday evening saw their chess game replaced with a solemn session of recitation and writing not unlike centuries ago when the oral poetry of one man was captured on the page by another.

Emilio read Sabines's words as if incanting a prayer. Alfredo honoured his friend's humility by producing his neatest calligraphy—not too flowery, not too severe. He used his finest fountain pen and the best quality black ink he could find. Emilio had contributed the paper—thick creamy vellum so thick Alfredo's nib had to deeply scratch the words of the Sabines's poem 'My love, my dear,' into it.

Once the scribing process was complete, Emilio watched the ink dry, declining the offer of a chess game as all his concentration was consumed by these magical words. He had requested no signature to be put below the poem, intending the words to stand alone in their own space without the claims of a poet.

Alfredo soon departed his friend's company, heading to his caravan to practice his vihuela to the point of perfection before the next day's performance, leaving Emilio alone. Folding the precious page into equal thirds, Emilio slipped it inside its envelope nest. It was only then he realised he'd forgotten to ask Alfredo to address the envelope to Lillibet. Like a lovesick teenager he had written out her name innumerable times during long solitary evenings. He could do so again. The pen wobbled in his hand but with supreme concentration he completed the name of his beloved, the letters only slightly sloping and uneven. The task he had imagined for so long was complete. His love for Lillibet had been captured by a letter. All that was left now was to secretly deliver this missive.

*

Lillibet was irritable before the evening's match. *What if my lifts falter tonight? Will my timing be on point? Will I bounce from the ropes with enough propulsion to jettison her off balance? What if the audience aren't on my side tonight? What if? What if?* Such doubts were usual; her nerves often manifested in this scratchiness, which Pilar was expected to absorb. To soothe and cajole her into a steadier state was one of Pilar's unending thankless tasks.

Fans had been arriving at the auditorium since five o' clock, clutching their gaudy masks tightly. The heat of the day still lingering. Rising from the earth beneath their feet, ready to receive the purple sun as it kissed the horizon. The spectators, though eager to engage in the collective spectacle, were nevertheless not naïve enough to encase their heads in their snugly fitting satin masks too soon. Best to hang on until the action.

An increasing number of women and girls attended matches in recent months. Even more on the increase were groups of young women happy and confident in the company of their friends. The slightly older generation of women quietly watched their exuberance and freedom with envy, sometimes questioning the life choices they had accepted. There were younger women looking casual in an ensemble of faded blue jeans and tight-fitting t-shirts that had taken hours to style. Others wore their outfits more consciously; flared cotton summer dresses printed with swirls of flowers ten times brighter than the brightest summer's morning. Their sandals were coordinated with their small, neat handbags, which were coordinated with their shade of lipstick. Maria, had she been there to witness, would have described them as 'well put together.'

There was a growing trend that amid these girls and women it was usual to find increasing smatterings of cholitas. They rarely fraternised with those in western outfits, but an air of mutual acceptance pervaded, tricky to define but present. A camaraderie. Those in western dress knew better than to patronise the cholitas with condescending approval. They observed them as they would exotic creatures in bright plumage, creatures who carried themselves with an air of surety typical of those who embodied both modernity and ancestry.

The weight of representation sat heavily on Lillibet's shoulders before each match. Not only did she wrestle athletically and gracefully, but had so, so many eyes of scrutiny on her. A regular male contingent within each audience disapproved of her—not only as a woman in the wrestling ring, but also as a cholita. 'She should better know her place,' they would echo backwards and forwards without a smidgen of self-reflection. That place being in the shadows, away from the cities, from public display. A place of subservience. These opinions had long been held by characters who not only judge, but unquestionably assume their right to do so. They are omnipresent, walking everywhere in plain sight. And their desire, perverse hope, for Lillibet was for her to falter. Even better, to perform in ways exposing a lack of talent, heralding a crushing of self-esteem. For them, she and others like her should retreat into the fog of humility and shame where these women belonged.

Another contingent of her audience watched her every match, willing her every throw, her every fall to be perfectly executed. Through her they had gained the legitimacy to be their true selves. She was a role model of the highest profile. The highest expectations. And if she faltered their own ascendancy may be threatened.

It was impossible for Lillibet to be unaware of the extent to which she had become a vehicle through which so many young women channelled their emotions. It was a heavy and intense weight. It made her irritable.

*

Lillibet allowed Pilar to brush out her hair, tangled from the afternoon's siesta. The weight of the brush against her scalp and the slow drawing of bristles through her hair evoked childhood evenings when Consuelo teased out her knots and brushed in sleepiness between the rituals of bath time and bedtime. It soothed her nervous energy even now. Today Pilar used long slow strokes. She was no fool.

In another caravan, Emilio and Emiliano were also preparing for the evening's match. Emilio as always had to resist being baited by his brother. He knew that between them he had to be the bigger man; failing to cooperate as a team in the ring would be their downfall. They needed to be sure their performance was so tight not even a sigh could slide between them.

Pre-match preparations were truly in motion across the troupe—the importance of ritual and symbolism, ever present. Even those scornful of superstition succumbing to lucky pants, ancient coins blessed by ancestors, and the small body parts of tiny animals—a rabbit's foot, the tail of a guinea pig. Emilio's ritual was to sit peacefully in quiet meditation, while his brother disturbed the air with star jumps and squats, pumping oxygen around his blood supply.

Today, meditating, Emilio grappled with anticipation.

He held onto his precious envelope, resting his hand in his lap—the one with the magical word 'Lillibet' written on it. This was the day his wooing would begin in earnest. 'Five, six, seven, eight,' cheered Emiliano as the caravan reverberated to his jumps. His brother merely inhaled and exhaled. Slowly.

*

Each wrestling event was as tightly choreographed as each individual match. The pervasive atmosphere of riot and recklessness was contained within a timetable exacted with tight precision. Nothing could be left to chance. Such tight choreography was exactly what was required to enable the lover to enact his secret mission. Emilio knew there would be a period of 35 minutes available to him after the completion of his initial match when Lillibet would be either backstage or in the ring. 35 minutes to wipe himself dry of his wrestler's sweat, run from the arena to his caravan, seize the envelope (carefully), run over the trodden grass to Lillibet and Pilar's caravan, deliver his missive, and return backstage with his absence unnoticed.

Emiliano's perpetual showing off always left his brother meandering in the shadows. This was usually a source of resentment, for Emilio, but on this evening it would play to his advantage. *He will be attracting the spotlight, making a spectacle of himself, showing off, and so I will be able to flow freely in the shadows.* Knowing that even if his brief absence was noticed, no one would for one moment suspect that he was undertaking a mission in the name of love.

A subtle smile of anticipatory joy flickered across his features. Even Emiliano's provocative poking and prodding didn't aggravate him this evening. Emilio was a cool, calm lover. Exactly the sort of man Lillibet needed by her side.

The enactment of the plan commenced at 9:21pm. The twins had easily won their first tag match against the Mighty Mountains. The audience had loved them—even the Mighty Mountain supporters had disloyally switched sides and cheered the twins. After their lap of victory, their arms raised to embrace the whoops of the crowd, their run around the perimeter of the ropes almost lapsing into a taunting dance, the minis tumbled out of the auditorium, exchanging high fives with the master of ceremonies in a display of mutual celebration, and a conspiratorial wink for those sitting in the front row.

Emilio smiled as he grabbed his towel and wiped his rounded belly and sweaty shoulders, slipping on his favourite t-shirt. He was not averse to creating a new superstition! The cloth adhered irritatingly to the heat of his back, but never mind. Shoes were not necessary; his feet were accustomed to the terrain—his soles had long been hardened into leather. He was ready to fly—his soul as light and tender as a butterfly. All omens were good: the setting sun providing him both respite from the heat and the welcomed hazy cover of dusk.

At 9:24pm he was primed, ready to undertake his mission. First step: enter his caravan to collect the precious envelope. 9:26pm: completed.

Second step: arrival at Lillibet's caravan. Having practised this transition many times under the disguise of training, he knew the sprint would take him between 92 and 96 seconds. Today, propelled by adrenaline, he shaved eight seconds off his personal best.

But then, as all good plans do when executed in real time, it faltered. The door to Lillibet's caravan was locked. Tight! He rattled it. Still locked. He shook it. Still locked. *They never usually lock their doors—what's going on!* Yet the lock felt flimsy as he gripped the handle. *It's not sitting securely in its case, it's not wedged. I can do this. I can do this.* A fleeting thought—one quick wrench would pull it open, and he would be inside faster than the speed of light. Thankfully, good sense washed over him, and his mind conjured the potential consequences: Lillibet and Pilar returning to their caravan weary amid their post-match energy drop, discovering the scene of a break in, an invasion of their sanctuary. This is hardly going to make Lillibet's heart conducive to receiving my words of love, even in the great Sabines's beautifully crafted words. *No, I either need to abort (for today) or find another way in.*

9.33pm. The clock was ticking.

Emilio's palms were perspiring. As he wiped them on his shorts he lamented their stickiness. Just then, a thought like a cartoon lightbulb occurred. Sticky hands. Cheaply made windows. The perfect combination for an ethical break in.

A quick look over each shoulder to ensure the absence of any stray passer-by and it was game on. He went round to the back of the caravan and found a rock to stand on. Deep breath. He placed his hands flat against the windowpane and allowed his sweat to do its work. His palms adhered and the windowpane slid like a hot knife through soft butter. Result!

What's that? There's a rustling in the bushes at the back. Is someone there? He hesitated, glanced and made direct eye contact with a solitary raccoon. Immobilised, they each stared, glassy eyed with the other, then with a mutual nod of recognition continued their own business.

If by chance a person taking a sunset stroll around the caravan park should have happened to wander amongst the dark shadows at the periphery, they would have spotted a small man silhouetted by the light of the rising gibbous moon, utilising his whole upper body strength to lift himself to a height from which he could roll through a caravan window and land on the floor below with an ungainly thud. What would not have been visible was the joyous sense of victory and relief on this man's face.

9.35pm.

Emilio patted his pocket. *Its okay, the envelope is still safely tucked away. Breathe.* He removed it and while carefully smoothing the creases caused by all of the limbering and rolling he also relaxed the creases on his forehead, causing a correlating drop in his shoulders. *Nearly there now.* He had by chance landed in Lillibet's bedroom and inhaled her lingering scent. He was tempted to touch and inhale her knick-knacks and clothes thrown on the bed—the items she herself had probably touched this day. *Don't lose focus.* He did however allow himself the indulgence of sinking his face into the soft fabric of a silk scarf flirtatiously framing one side of the mirror. He breathed her in, then exhaled a delicious sigh. His next task was to calmly lay the envelope on her pillow; he stepped back and examined the positioning, confirming his precious envelope was unmissable. The white envelope shone against the pink pillowcase. Yet still he straightened it, again, then shifted it once more to a slight tilt. *Job done*

Emilio, job done. I just need to get back unnoticed.

'Where have you been? It's quarter to and we're back on in 20 minutes,' spat Emiliano as his brother returned to the changing rooms, a telltale smudge of mud across his cheek.

'Twenty minutes is ages,' replied Emilio with a newly found calm. 'Lots can be achieved in 20 minutes.'

'What are you being so cryptic about? And wipe that smug look and that mud off your face. Just because we won the first match today doesn't mean we'll win the next. Get yourself changed; you look as if you've been rolling through long grass.'

Normally Emiliano's temperament would get under Emilio's skin, connecting him with those years of sleights that had always come thick, never allowing time for scabs to form over the emotional wounds. But somehow, this evening, nothing could upset his equilibrium—his mind was truly elsewhere, in a place full of joy and promise.

*

Emiliano had hoped Lillibet would join the party crowd that evening—there was a big night planned. A night of fun and revelry. He had been practising jokes in a bid to attract her attention. Alas he had to concede disappointment as she politely declined invitations from other members of the troupe, excusing herself with a claim of weariness and maybe a headache threatening to tighten her temples. She dismissed Pilar with an impatient flick of her wrist, 'You go out and have fun if you like. Don't worry, I can fix my own supper.'

'If you're sure,' her friend faltered. 'Supper is already made. It's in the fridge. You just need to warm it through.'

'Yes, go and have fun,' snapped Lillibet.

Pilar was unsure of the cause of Lillibet's brittleness. Was it post-match tiredness or the growing resentment of her own blossoming social life? This itchiness between them was becoming an increasingly frequent companion in their relationship. She knew they should talk, discuss what was causing such a schism. Pilar was aware, however, that she would have to initiate such a conversation. *Another day*, she promised herself. *Another day*. Instead, she graciously closed this exchange with a kiss on each of her friend's cheeks.

'Sleep well my darling. I'll see you when you wake tomorrow morning.'

'Yes,' muttered Lillibet, already pulling away.

Despite her headache looming, Lillibet slammed the caravan door once Pilar left. She knew she was being unreasonable, unkind, and yet she felt unable to stop. Why can't I take joy in my friend's happiness—she's my friend. Why does it feel like a desertion? She just didn't have the emotional resources to orchestrate this dialogue in her head. Instead, she slipped off her ballet slippers, jettisoned her hat and without the usual evening ritual of lighting the gas lanterns, went into her bedroom and threw herself on the bed. From outside filtered merriment and laughter, gradually fading into the distance as she closed her heavy eyelids.

A couple of hours later when she stirred, she noticed she felt both chilly and had been dribbling on her pillow. The corner of her room was startlingly bright. She lay still looking at the light cast by the moon hanging in a clear sky. All she longed for was to lie still and enjoy the peace while the carnival of her life was suspended. But the pressure on her bladder was too much. Annoyed at the disagreement between her body and psyche, she succumbed to the inevitable trip to the bathroom.

Her pee felt hot and smelt bitter. *I must remember to drink more water, take more care of myself.* In the five short steps it took to walk between bathroom and kitchen, Lillibet glanced into Pilar's room and noted the neatly made empty bed. Unsure about what time of night it was, she shrugged, not caring to consider the whereabouts of her friend. She wanted to sleep forever.

Gulping her third glass of water in quick succession she headed back to her bedroom, knowing she should shed her crumpled, sweat-stained clothes and slip into the beautifully laundered nightdress Pilar had left out for her. It all just felt like too much effort.

As she sank back into the comfort of her bed, she felt something unfamiliar beneath her shoulder blades. The object was flat and flimsy yet had sharp corners. Was it paper? She pulled it out and examined it. An envelope. An envelope with her name written on it in curious, unusual handwriting. Lillibet shuffled into the light of the moon rays, and with her index finger slid it open, releasing its contents like a fragile moth dancing against a midnight sky.

*

Saturday was Lucha Libre's last night in Xalapa—a magnificent town, deserving a big finale. And then a few days off to kick back, relax, soak sore muscles, repair costumes, catch breath. Before the rest and relaxation, however, tonight would be party night.

Pilar was surprised, on waking, that the day began with an unexpected encounter with Lillibet in the kitchen. The caravan door was already flung open, inviting dancing rays of sunshine. The radio was pumping dance music and all the kitchen surfaces were awash with a melee of cooking utensils, spilt flour, cracked eggshells and random items of cutlery fraternising unashamedly. And amid this Lillibet swirled in her favourite fuchsia and purple strappy nightdress, tresses swinging as their owner appeared to be dancing breakfast pancakes into being.

Pilar had to raise her voice a pitch higher than the blaring radio to get her friend's attention.

'Ah Pilar,' echoed the whirlwind without lowering the volume of the radio or indeed the volume of her transmission.

'You're late arising. You've already missed too much of this glorious day!' *Whisk, bang, crack* went the kitchen utensils. 'Coffee?' It wasn't so much a question as an announcement, as a mug of dark steaming liquid emitting a seductive aroma was placed in her hands. 'Do you want lemon or orange juice on your pancakes?'

'Are you okay?' asked Pilar tentatively. Accustomed to her morning ritual of trying to entice Lillibet out of her dishevelled bed—akin to luring a bat out of a darkened cave at noon on a summer's day—this was all unsettling.

'Sorry honey, what did you say?' shouted Lillibet over the disco beat.

Pilar quickly decided a strategy of acceptance rather than questioning was best. The whirlwind was expelling the excess of stale energy accumulated in the caravan over the previous weeks.

'Lemon please. Lemon juice on my pancakes.'

*

As sensitive to changes in vibrations in the atmosphere as a tuning fork is to the resonance of sound, Pilar embodied her maternal lineage: her grandmother was a healer. Her first memory, her first sense of awe, was bearing witness to the villagers presenting themselves to Grandma when their spirits were out of kilter. As a child Pilar would watch as with a quiet dignity her elder soothed these spirits with the laying on of hands, subsequently sending newly calmed people back into the world. Her mother, in contrast, was a more pragmatic woman, given to maintaining domestic warmth and harmony, providing Pilar the material comforts of life—cushions embroidered with love and sauces cooked to delicate perfection. A precious, warm heart that emitted love to all within and beyond her household.

Pilar had inherited these qualities, either through her genes or absorption. Whatever the route, the result was the same—she empathised with others, experiencing pleasure, sorrow, frustration, and humour keenly when those around her did. There was no exception when attuning to Lillibet's fluctuating energies.

Pilar looked on endlessly as Lillibet's natural charisma drew in those within her orbit and centrifugally swirled them with whatever emotion she was channelling at any moment. Well-meaning folk had at times tentatively suggested meditation to Lillibet, as a vehicle to regulate her erratic nature. She had given it a go. Twice. But found it too passive, became too frustrated, and so any further suggestions were dismissed. 'I've tried that. It doesn't work.'

But today, Lillibet's buoyant mood was infectious. Pilar greeted this with a tentative welcome. To her it was as if the scene outside the caravan wasn't merely reflecting Lillibet's mood, but that Lillibet was evoking it. The air was so clear sound was travelling without inhibitions. The laughter of fellow wrestlers could be heard as they greeted each other and acknowledged today as a holiday before their wheels would roll them ever onwards to a new town, a new crowd. Two cuckoos were playing serve and return with their mating calls, interspersed by the wheezing of an accordion flexed and contracted by an amateur player to greet the new day.

Meanwhile, Pilar felt unsure if the smell of frangipani was coming from a nearby tree, or if Lillibet had squirted herself with perfume. It was heady, overwhelming. The perfection of the scene only intruded on by the irritating buzz of a misplaced fly, but that too curtailed as it cruelly became trapped to the stickiness of the yellow adhesive strip dangling by the window.

Despite the sounds of people rising from their beds, there were few folks visible. Pilar noticed Emilio as he passed their caravan, peering in on them. Maybe he too had been compelled by the joyful whirlwind of Lillibet cooking. Pilar waved a good morning to him as he raised a tentative hand in response before hurrying on his way.

Enjoying the morning bathed in a warm glow, Emilio had noticed Lillibet's happy mood from afar, had heard the melodious sounds from the caravan, and was now spurred in his quest to win her heart. He assumed her joy was as a direct result of being the chosen recipient of his note. He assumed correctly.

Although a man with poetry in his soul, Emilio was, deep down, like most of us, a logical thinker. So his sequential thought train followed as thus:

If one poem from me makes her happy...
then more poems from me will make her even happier
if she realises that I can make her happy...
then she will want to be with me, always.
if she wants to be with me always...
then I will live my life as a happy, contented man.

Lillibet was less prone to such analytical thoughts; the nature of her personality more spontaneous and present. Some people had even been known to describe her as reactive.

Both traits were in part what made Emilio and Lillibet excellent wrestlers—the ability to predict the opponent's tactics and moves and thereby thwart them. But would these traits also make them compatible lovers? Meanwhile Pilar, unaware of the developing narrative, was content, savouring not only the lightness of the early morning but the slightly overcooked pancakes that tasted of optimism.

*

Emiliano was too caught in his own ego to contemplate that Lillibet's brightness of smile and lightness of foot was to do with anyone but himself. He would never in a month of Sundays have guessed it had anything to do with his brother. Neither would Lillibet have guessed her current buoyancy was about Emilio. But that's another matter. Emiliano sighed deeply from his heart as he watched the playful antics of a passing squirrel and indulged his own reflections… *Yesterday evening I was able to chat with her for a short time alone. Between our bouts in the ring we found ourselves lingering outside the arena getting air (I went in search of her but for now she thinks it was a chance encounter). Fortunately, Emilio was nowhere, so I was unencumbered by the dull analysis he indulges after a match. It was just me and her. She and I. And I could show her my true self: I cracked my best well-rehearsed jokes; she laughed. I pointed out constellations in the night sky—she was captivated. I told her of our latest victory in the ring—she showered me with praise, like the aurora of a shooting star. It was the chance I've been waiting for to prove that there is more to me than just the fun guy she sees in the bar. And I could feel a connection. The vibes were strong. I know she didn't hang around for drinks later, but I no longer need to impress her as part of the group—she sees the true me. And then this morning when I heard the tinkling of her laughter filling the air, dancing in harmony with the rising birdsong, I could tell her heart was filling with excitement, anticipation. I'm on my way to making her mine.*

These thoughts rumbled through his ego as he walked past the women's caravan. It was a vortex that morning, drawing energy into its centre. Emiliano circumnavigated it three times and rather than rippling out he was drawn, with a force beyond his control, to the heart of things. He decided he may as well surrender to fate.

'Knock, knock,' said Emiliano, verbalising the sound his knuckles made on the open caravan door.

'There's a lot of merriment coming from here this morning. Are you excited about us moving on tomorrow? We'll be in Tuxtia to watch the sunset. We had such a great time there last year—the bars are great, and the street food is amazing.'

There was a pause as if his presence had subdued the atmosphere like a parent walking into a teenage party. Surely, he wasn't an intruder? He felt aware of his masculinity and how something was jarring, as if in a place he didn't belong. It reminded him of days in his childhood when he would arrive home from school and enter a domestic scene of Maria and a couple of women neighbours sat around an array of half empty cups on the kitchen table, crochet wool and hooks on their laps. The lightness in the air would stall when he entered, the women exchanging looks that magically silenced each other. Maria would, without fail, invent a spurious errand for him, his departure heralding tinkling laughter—the same quality of laughter he had heard tumbling out of Lillibet and Pilar's caravan just before his arrival, or intrusion.

Lillibet broke the awkwardness with a cryptic, curious question: 'Oh Emiliano. It is not the bars and streets we're anticipating, but the poetry. Tell me, will we find any poets in Tuxtia?'

He thought she had winked at him. He may have been mistaken. This sense of floundering in a verbal exchange was disorientating, but there had been a seismic shift in Lillibet's tone he hadn't anticipated nor could comprehend. Emiliano was a man who, despite his light-hearted public persona, liked clarity. If only the world could just travel forever forwards in a straight line without deviation: being awash in a sea of ambiguity and nuance was too much to handle. Should he steer the exchange to a safe shore, or retreat and regroup, compose himself? The latter wasn't his style—consequently he took a deep breath. This breath, trapped in his throat, was infiltrated with a metallic taste. *Is this what mercury tastes of?*

It didn't feel right. He had lost too much of his inherent power which he knew drew Lillibet towards him. Why was she so suddenly talking of poets? They had never gone looking for poets in a town before, why now? Something was off kilter, not least his ability to speak. He swallowed a lump of sticky saliva. Should he retreat? Regroup? Only show himself to her at his best? *Yes, yes, yes* shouted a voice from deep inside. Was this what intuition felt like?

Lillibet's mouth was fixed in a smile, but the rest of her face was a little twisted.

'Is everything alright Emiliano? You've gone quiet.'

'Fine, fine, everything is just fine. Just fine. But I've remembered that I have to be in… I have to… I have to go.'

Lillibet watched the departing figure as he exited their caravan and scurried. How strange. What had just happened? Maybe this was how poets were when they revealed their true selves. It was all such unfamiliar territory. With a shrug she poured more pancake batter into the pan, 'Why not have this one with honey Pilar?'

*

They arrived in Tuxtia at dusk. The wrestlers were at heart nomads, troubadours, wanderers who found comfort in movement. They all experienced an excess of energy and for some an inability to still their minds. So the fresh stimulus of a new town, new people, a fresh landscape, and unfamiliar smells created a collective rumble of pervasive curiosity.

Children, thrilled by anticipation mixed with the pleasure of the exotic, ran alongside the river of caravans, heels kicking up dust as they waved and squealed. The wrestlers, the embodiment of their dreams of escape to a life of excitement and risk, had entered their little backwater. For real. Teenage girls loitered on street corners and in shop doorways in groups of three or four, feigning disinterest, pretending their street presence at the precise time the entourage waltzed through town was coincidental. Nevertheless their gazes lingered after the carnival in the hope of glimpsing Lillibet. Some harboured secret fantasies that this beautiful creature may meet their gaze, and there might be recognition, a shared bond between a girl who longed to harness her inner strength and release it into the world, with the woman who embodied this very thing. She had once been one of them, and she had made it. This possibility would prove just enough to sustain the girls through their turbulent teenage years in a claustrophobic small town.

As for Emilio, new towns unnerved him, having become used to the previous place, having established daily routines that allowed him to carve out quiet spaces. In each new town he had to begin the process anew. Today, however, felt different—he too felt anticipation brewing deep within like the rising bubbles in a boiling saucepan. This morning he had persuaded Alfredo to scribe another of Sabines's poems for him. Or more accurately, for Lillibet. Not a whole poem, but a stanza he had pored over and over some more until selecting the words that most closely conveyed his love. In turn, these words had been beautifully copied by his friend, onto a fresh sheet of delicious cream notepaper. It was then carefully folded, now into quarters with crisp edges and finally tucked inside another tissue paper-lined envelope. Emilio patted his pocket at regular intervals to ensure the ongoing presence of his precious cargo. His mission to execute a fresh delivery—one mission, despite meticulous planning, had been lucky; the second ran a greater risk. But maybe subconsciously this is what his heart desired.

Emiliano had spent most of this journey playing Siete Loco with Gabriel, tucked at the back of the bus, the windows firmly shut and blinds pulled in the reek of unshowered masculinity. As they slowed through traffic he extricated himself from the group as a new round was dealt, bustled down the bus aisle and plonked himself in the seat next to Emilio, jolting his brother out of his pleasant reverie.

'I want to introduce a new move into our sequence. I want us to practise the Burning Hammer so we can surprise folks. Shake things up a bit.'

The few seconds it took Emilio to shift his thoughts into this unforeseen announcement was enough to evoke impatience in his brother.

'Well, say something! Why can't you share my enthusiasm? This is a brilliant idea. Only the best wrestlers execute the Burning Hammer; everyone knows how dangerous it is. People are going to love us more and more.'

Little did Emilio realise that by 'people' his brother meant Lillibet. Emiliano couldn't, at that point, care less what the public thought of them. And the prize he was aiming for wasn't the money or glory. His target for admiration was so much more focused.

At this point Emilio was blinkered to the idea that he may not be Lillibet's sole suitor. Being so absorbed in his own courtship ritual, he overlooked the most obvious fact—Lillibet was an engaging, attractive, single young woman. To anyone not consumed in the headiness of love, anyone with a clear, logical mind, it was predictable others would want to get close to her too. Close to her mind, and to her body. Not only was she strong and beautiful, but a rising star, and, goodness knows, so many desire closeness to fame and fortune. As if it may transfer to themselves by magic.

*

In tracking and reporting their every move, the national media whipped up a frenzy heralding the luchadores' arrival at each town. Tickets sold out weeks in advance and were now touted, gifted, and resold all over. In bars, offices and at school gates people speculated about dalliances between members of the troupe, fantasising that the intensity of training sessions in hot steamy halls led to liaisons in hot steamy bedrooms. It satiated the compulsive drive of gamblers as bets were placed left, right and centre, some more officially. Children had undertaken school projects, spilling beyond the confines of the classrooms into imitations of their heroes in playgrounds. Elders had dusted off their own wrestling masks and relished recounting stories which although varied and meandering, always began: 'I remember way back when I...'

Lillibet's skin had a plump glow and her eyes were a sparkle. The tightness she held in knotted muscles in her shoulders for the past few weeks was dissolving by the hour, which in turn elongated her neck and raised her chin with imperiousness. Standing proud and comfortable, her radiance cast a dull shadow on all within her orbit.

Emiliano knew he had to make his move before anyone else. As his fellow drinking pals said of the women they preyed on, he had to 'get in there'. But what was this recent glow about? Was it his imagination or was she looking even more delicious than usual? No matter—what was more important than such bellybutton gazing was for him to seize her before another man.

Lillibet, curiously, wasn't aware she was a prize to be won. She was just herself. But these days more so.

The troupe arrived and made camp. Some folks had wandered off to catch the late afternoon tail end of the market, partly to stock up on food supplies and partly to get a feel of the local atmosphere. Emiliano located a log conveniently placed near but not too near Lillibet and Pilar's caravan spot. He sat a while, burrowing a hole in the dusty earth with the heel of his trainers while watching the shadows of the two women set about making a new home from home. Songs from their radio carried across the still air. Emiliano wasn't used to sitting still; the nervous energy pulsing through his body as a child had never been tamed. This restlessness wasn't always a great quality outside of the ring—an emotion entered his heart and before he could anchor it, his body sprung into action. Impulsive, reactive.

He kicked stones into a dust hole, stood and straightened his crumpled t-shirt. *Don't back out like last time. Cowardice will get you nowhere.* His line of vision like a taut rope, he ran directly towards his love. Or at least her caravan door. His swift knock was met by an equally swift opening of the door as an expectant Pilar called out: 'Welcome Gabriel.' Her mouth dropped in disappointment. Being a kind soul though, she quickly composed her features into a smile.

'Emiliano. How nice to see you at our door again. Are you okay? How can we help you?'

'Don't be so formal, Pilar,' called out Lillibet from behind her. 'First, invite our guest in, offer him a nice cold drink and a seat and then find out why we've been honoured with a visit. Unless he's come to inform us of a fire or the threat of a volcanic eruption, and that we're in mortal danger!'

Pilar stepped aside and with an exaggerated flourish of her arm, welcomed him into this inner sanctum. Emiliano felt a little rush of excitement chase through his chest cavity. With a faster heartbeat than was comfortable he stepped into the room that served the women as a sitting room and kitchen.

'Take a seat Emiliano,' chimed Lillibet as she shifted a small mountain of dresses and petticoats discarded on the window seat. Beneath the vibrant dresses he noticed the seat was padded in flowered purple and orange linen. Everything looked so welcoming in this caravan, different from his own.

'Put the kettle on please Pilar,' she called to her friend in a tone far too loud considering the compactness of the space.

Emiliano slid into the seat and rested his elbows on the fold out table, wishing his feet reached the floor rather than dangling and swinging despite attempts to exert control over them.

'To what do we owe the pleasure of your visit today?' asked Lillibet with mock formality. 'I think this is the second time you've ever visited our abode before, isn't it Pilar?'

Despite the door being slightly ajar Emiliano was aware of the acrid smell of Calor gas fuelling the flame beneath the kettle. He couldn't quite locate the source of this claustrophobia pressing on him. Maybe it was the overriding sense of oestrogen in this confined space; everything so feminine—the décor, clothes, smells, the women's presence. It was all too much. He wanted to balance it out—inject testosterone into the mix. *Why have I come here so spontaneously, so unprepared?* He still couldn't shake the feeling that unless he acted in a very deliberate way, he might lose Lillibet, even though he was yet to win her.

The silence, the gap between her question and his response became too long, too elongated. 'Looking forward to the matches tomorrow?' he blurted, then pushed both hands beneath his thighs and treated the women to a rictus grin.

They nodded. Was he imagining it or were they somewhat distracted—Pilar making tea and Lillibet straightening curtains and plumping cushions. A small knot of yearning gripped Emiliano's stomach and he felt his bowels rumble. The domesticity of the scene made his mind spring to Maria and he became acutely aware of just how long it had been since he gave her so much as a thought, never mind a letter or a phone call. His mind grappled to form a sharp image of her kitchen: were the curtains red and white checked, or maybe orange and blue? And did she still have that sofa with the sunken springs? Were the rugs on the floor of the front room greenish, or was that the kitchen rugs?

Pilar placed a teapot and three chunky ceramic red mugs on the table. As she turned to find the sugar and spoons, Lillibet slid into the seat opposite Emiliano and shone a bright smile upon him. The configuration of table and seats reminded him of being aboard a train: an image quickly formed of himself and Lillibet on window seats, embarking on a joint adventure. Just them. Maybe their first holiday, or even honeymoon. He was acutely aware they'd never had their faces in such close, focused proximity—close enough that if one of them were to lean forward inches they could kiss for the first time. He saw that her green eyes had small spots of brown flecks, scattered randomly like a forest floor. This, he realised, was his chance to impress her.

'Have you heard the joke about the wolf and the boy?' His mind screamed 'Noooooo!'

A slight frown crossed Lillibet's brow.

'...the joke about the wolf...' Lillibet tailed. 'Aren't you here to deliver an envelope? I won't ask you the name of the sender I promise, because obviously that would spoil the fun,' she teased, a slight red flush framing her cheekbones.

He noticed her pupils dilate and sensed they were mirroring his. As she spoke, she absent-mindedly rubbed the leaves of the verbena plant sitting decoratively on the formica table between her thumb and forefinger. She smelt her lemon-scented fingertips and nodded approvingly. Stretching her tanned arm across the table she offered her fingers to Emiliano to share the olfactory pleasure. To reach he had to raise himself, pressing his forearms into the table. Her upper body leant forwards so he could inhale the scent reminiscent of lemon bonbons. It was heady, conjuring rare times during his childhood, when if she had a small amount of spare cash Maria would surprise the twins with gifts of small paper cones of sticky sweets. These he crushed between his back teeth while Emilio savoured their flavour, sucking each in turn for an eternity.

As Lillibet reached forward, her arm compressed her right breast which in turn raised higher, pushing at the stretched edges of her sundress. He gazed at the fullness of her flesh; he was so close he could see the open pores on her skin releasing drops of perspiration. *If only this moment could last forever.* Sadly she withdrew her arm and her glorious breast retreated into her dress. Emiliano instinctively grabbed hold of her wrist, her tendons taut. In comparison his hand was small and unable to circumnavigate her wrist. Nevertheless, he managed to hold her body in a freeze frame—except for her left eyebrow arched into a question mark.

'Are you looking for an arm wrestle little fella?'

'Not exactly.' As he held her wrist she held his gaze.

'I'd take you down with one swipe.' Was it bravado or something more nuanced, more intimate?

'I doubt it,' refuted Emiliano. 'There's a lot more to this body of mine than meets the eye.' He was careful to lace his smile with reassuring warmth.

'Pilar, Pilar. Where is my love?' The moment was broken by Gabriel poking his head through the caravan window. Lillibet and Emiliano dropped their arms, releasing their mutual grip as if dropping hot coals.

'Oh I say, am I disturbing something?' blundered the Skeleton.

'You were disturbing my cup of tea,' replied Lillibet, her line of vision focused on the view from the window, on her cup, on the table—anywhere other than where Emiliano sat.

'Our caravan feels like the village square at times with all sorts of people dropping in without invitation. Haven't you both got anything better to do?' There was an audible full stop at the end of that question. Lillibet stood, brushed invisible crumbs from her skirt, picked up carrots from the vegetable basket and scrubbed the soil from them, studiously avoiding anyone's eyes.

*

When Emiliano replayed this scene over and over in his mind that evening, he was certain Gabriel had dropped him a wink of comradeship just before he playfully wriggled his snakelike body through the window with a sound of bones banging against the stainless-steel window frame. Or had he imagined it? Had Gabriel observed that moment of tenderness and read it for what he was sure it was—the beginning of a great love affair.

*

Miguel sat in a battered camping chair outside the arena wondering exactly how he'd arrived here. He hadn't intentionally embarked on this series of stepping stones laying a path across the river, any river, neither a literal nor metaphorical one. But somehow, he had ended so far away from home it instilled vertigo in him. It had all transpired via small incremental steps fuelled by minor decisions, which he had no impression then of their collective consequences. And now here he was, so far away... literally and metaphorically.

He cast his mind to the day Lillibet and Pilar came to the gym, full of fake bravado, to ask him to teach them to wrestle. If he was to trace his journey to a starting point this would be it. A starting point only imbued with such weight of meaning in retrospect. It wasn't as if someone had fired a gun or foreboding music played on the radio in the background to warn him of the foreshadowing of events. But had Miguel turned down the requests from these bold young women on that day they sashayed in, then he wouldn't find himself here, in a dilapidated town so far from all that was familiar.

Think of the money, think of the money—that is coming in handy. His parents, his closely guarded secret, were no longer living each week hand to mouth. Since his father's accident, his inability to work and their consequent descent into poverty, only temporarily buffered from destitution by their meagre savings, life had been tough. This recent security his proteges provided Miguel didn't feel like his birthright. It was a temporary state, a brief interlude. All that needed to happen was for Lillibet to be injured and he would again find himself and his parents eking a living training wrestlers of an evening and using his carpentry skills to build simple, functional furniture during the daily working hours and long into dusk filled evenings. His fate had become intrinsically linked with Lillibet. If she rose, he rose. If she fell, his fate would also tumble.

As his mind gravitated towards falling and tumbling, an awareness dawned that injury wasn't the only event to jeopardise himself and his protégé. She was now at an age when the distraction of love affairs, even pregnancy, would be possible. A tumble in an unmade bed could lead to their mutual downfall. He drew sharply on his cigar, contemplating the improbability of this happening. He secretly admired her, though best not to let her know: he needed to maintain authority as her coach! He was aware, though, that she was uncompromising in her refusal to live her life in the male shadow: she did not define herself in relation to men, not her father, not her brothers, nor even himself. She was a woman capable of creating and occupying her own spotlight.

He stubbed the nub of his cigar with his leather boot and gazed at the arid, dry earth. How had he gotten here? And more importantly, how could he regain his self-sustainability?

*

Lucha libre wasn't merely a sport or piece of theatre. It was magic—a temporary fantasy (for what other sort of fantasy is there?). An escape from the mundanity of day-to-day life. The audience could suspend disbelief for just over three hours, allowing themselves to be seduced into a binary simplicity. They could pin their angst and fears on the rudos, who prowled the perimeter of the ring hissing at the jeering audience. And when the technicos triumphed, that same audience could then believe that ultimately in this world, good will prevail. Justice will always be done. The light will drive out the dark. If we just hold fast to our moral compass.

The audience, adorned in masks, so much more than passive observers: they were part of the spectacle. So much some would blink in disbelief when the wrestlers took their final bows, the house lights were reilluminated and they found themselves again back outside the arena and firmly in their mundane reality.

The wrestlers insisted that at each arena there was the magical portal of heavy crimson velvet curtain through which they could make their entrances—a signifier the world over of the separation between reality and fantasy. When these curtains are raised in theatres, the audience expects to be transported on the play's journey of the imagination. Similar curtains are parted as the sex worker leads the punter by the hand into the secret room within the depths of the brothel, a room of escapism and pleasure.

Stopping to show off their plumage of capes and boots, masks and shorts, shawls and petticoats, their shimmer always caught in the spotlight. Cymbals would clash to announce the commencement of the merriment. Unleash the dogs of war, it was time for battle. And later, when battle was done, all energy spent, it was through the heavy velvetiness the wrestlers departed with a raised fist and a comradely wave from the technicos or a final snarl from the rudos. The projection of shadows and dreams—the fantasy of the extraordinary—was complete.

Reality must not impinge on fantasy lest the spell be broken. They were showmen. They were show-women. Maintaining the illusion, the wrestlers made sure never to be seen in their costumes outside the arena—they would wander in market places, in malls and on the streets in the safety of groups, always masked, always mysterious. And playing their role in unison, the public would whoop and cry at the delight of magic invading their everyday lives.

At each venue the wrestlers set up changing rooms where they could de-costume, wipe off the greasepaint, disrobe out of their magical capes, sweep aside the sequins. Transform themselves back to mere mortals. It really wouldn't do for a member of the public to spot a masked hero slipping into the temporary home—a battered caravan standing in a dust bowl of a field.

Emiliano was riding high from his interaction with Lillibet. To have savoured her undivided attention in her caravan for a while had fired up his loins. To say nothing of what it had done for his imagination! He had attempted to catch her eye at the evening's finale—the glorious moment the wrestlers bathed in the audience's adoration. But while her body was present, perspiring from the exertion and the heat of the lights, a broad smile spreading across her face, she herself seemed absent. Emiliano checked he and his desires weren't being sussed by Miguel, but the coach was just sitting in the front row picking fragments of nuts out of his teeth. He too was elsewhere.

The troupe tumbled their exit through the velvet curtains, eager to change into their evening threads and explore the local drinking holes. As Emiliano walked past Lillibet's changing room he nodded to Gabriel, who had already disrobed from his skeleton costume, and was leaning his skinny frame against the door, tapping his left foot, waiting for Pilar to hurry up. Emiliano paused and the two men observed a tender moment between the two women, as Pilar unravelled the plaited curtain of her friend's hair. Lillibet sat quietly in front of a scratched mirror watching this nightly ritual with an air of absence. Emiliano nodded at the Skeleton. Gabriel nodded back. It was a now or never moment for Emiliano. He slid through the opening of the door, walked straight to the women and held Lillibet's gaze in the mirror.

'Why don't you grab your bag Pilar and go and have fun with Gabriel under the stars, I'll finish off helping Lillibet.'

He reached up and removed the hairbrush from Pilar's hand, who in her surprise readily relinquished it. Emiliano nodded his head in encouragement, sliding his gaze to Gabriel then back to Pilar. He gave her a broad grin, feigning confidence as if he were in complete control. Holding tight to the hairbrush despite his increasingly clammy palms, he silently muttered something between a wish and a prayer, *Please go... just go and leave me alone with her.*

A curious assortment of abandoned objects littered the room: boxes of various shapes and sizes, a clothes rack with dusty neglected coats dangling sadly, odd shoes that had given up the search for their mate, a large ceramic dog, and bunting hanging from the ceiling on a frayed string. What could he do? He needed an object to raise his height. *Ah yes, thank goodness*—he spotted an empty plastic milk crate. Perfect. With the tips of his toes he nudged it into position behind Lillibet's chair, upturned it and then with an explosive double footed jump, landed atop. From this position he could reach the top of Lillibet's head with the precision of a brain surgeon.

Hands reached: Gabriel extended his to Pilar as she acquiesced, slipping her hand into his bony yet reassuring grip. Emiliano tried to control the tremble passing through his hands. With his left held flat he caressed the sheen of Lillibet's hair with delight. In his right he clutched the tortoiseshell hairbrush, finding comfort like a baby clutching their mother's finger. Lillibet reached one hand to pick up her neglected glass of tonic water, leaving a sticky ring on the bench in front of her. Her gaze focused studiously on the glass, avoiding Emiliano's eyes in the mirror.

'I think you can stop,' she told him after twenty minutes of his long, sweeping brushes of her hair. She didn't want him to stop, but for him to continue felt too indulgent on her part. Or maybe on his. She couldn't tell for sure. Each time the bristles made contact with her scalp, Emiliano applied a little more pressure. Not too much—just a little. It reminded her of how as a child Consuelo would soothe her to sleep with similar motions.

The glide of the brush from follicle to hair tip felt like the motion of a smooth-running brook, with no rocks to hinder its flow. She longed to lie down and surrender. Bit-by-bit she allowed herself to watch Emiliano's mirror reflection, wondering how she had never observed such a tender side to this man. She smiled at his reflection, which smiled back. This surge opened a closely guarded river of vulnerability, a stream she felt must be blocked like a dam for fear of the tide flowing over too suddenly.

Eventually the spell broke. He climbed from his makeshift stool and placed the brush on the bench before her. It sat alongside objects he realised he hadn't seen since leaving Maria's home: makeup brushes, little soft rabbit tail orbs of cotton wool, red lipstick, blue eyeshadow glistening like sunlight on the ocean, and an octopus of tangled ribbons. The same objects had been a constant on his mother's dressing table, but her comb was made of black plastic, her unguents sat thickly in the bottom of scratched jars, and her lipstick was always worn down to a thin nub.

His reverie was broken by Lillibet standing, fidgeting, 'I must get going back to my caravan. I think I need an early night.'

Brush, brush went her hand over the creases in her skirt caused by the immobile sitting.

'Oh! Are you feeling okay?' he asked.

'Yes, I'm fine. I just want to rest. Thanks for doing my hair. See you tomorrow.'

In a whoosh of petticoats she was gone. Emiliano reached his hand out into the vacant space and grasped the air. An onlooker would have supposed he was either exercising his hand or trying to catch a flying insect.

*

When a day trip to the underground caves of Rio Secreto was suggested, the troupe were divided. Inevitably so. One camp were those who even on the brightest days—full of sunshine and birdsong and promise—were drawn into the darkness of the world's underbelly as if it held an ancestral memory. A magnetic pull that lures us back, to a place of safety from the threats of the woods' retreat. This camp asked: 'What time do we set off?' The others, however, replied with a firm 'No'. For them the caves held fear—the unmoving air is suffocating, the ceiling looms ever lower with the threat of collapse, driving them into the bowels of the earth. Ashes to ashes.

Some, regardless of their feelings towards this

underworld, preferred to spend their downtime just chilling: playing cards, setting the world to rights, or immersed in the domestic rituals of laundry, polishing windows with vinegar, paying cheques into the bank, settling the rent bill from home.

Miguel was the self-appointed troupe's trip researcher, coming up with the options each town and surrounding area offered well before they arrived. He would check opening times, ticket costs, transport routes. His motivation was never to go on these trips but to secure quiet days for himself while the others set off on his well-planned jaunts. One person's escape is another's retreat.

When the troupe headed out on an excursion, there was often a control issue: not a lack of it but an excess of those who wanted to take the helm. Wrestlers tend to be leaders rather than followers—always thrusting, ducking, diving to gain authority in the ring, asserting the self with ever-increasing forcefulness. What should have been lighthearted days out usually began with debates about the departure time, and by lunch had invariably spiralled into arguments about who should be first in the queue for the gift shop.

For this reason Emilio practised avoidance. Conflict made him edgy, uncomfortable—just the atmosphere it created, even if not directed at himself. He hated the sensation of the air around his becoming heavier and the associated slight strangulation in his breathing. Today though, today's prospect was different—it had a double attraction. First, he loved the quiet containment that caves provided, and second, Lillibet would be there.

It was on a Wednesday lunchtime when he found himself squashed in the middle of a group of muscular, sweaty wrestlers collectively marvelling at dust motes dancing in light shafts jutting through fissures in the earth's core.

'Hello.'

'Hello.'

'Hello.'

The call and return reverberated in the cavernous space until it was impossible to tell which voice belonged to the caller and which was the cave's reply.

The guide had long given up trying to do his job of imparting carefully researched historical facts and geological nuggets of information. As a logical man it was curious that people should be more interested in immersing themselves in a sense of mystery than learning truths. But each to their own. Their ticket price paid his wages.

'See how the light enters that crevice and bounces off the stone.'

'It feels like being deep, deep under the ocean.'

'Which gods do you think the cave dwellers prayed to?'

'Hello. Hello. Hello.'

An air of reverence hovered, typical of when humans find themselves in a place of natural wonder—the undeniable sense that nature has a pattern in which human understanding is only a chink. There is something bigger than our species, and maybe, just maybe, we are not as much in control of our destinies as we pretend. Humans are tiny; actors in a spinning universe.

As the group looked to the cathedralesque cave roof and marvelled at the chandelier cluster of stalactites, Emilio was easily able to weave through the group and position himself beside Lillibet. She stood, head tilted back, craning upwards. Her right hand ensured her bowler hat didn't fall backwards from the crown of her head, and her left hung by her side—the extension of her relaxed, limp arm. Her shoulders, in a holiday mood, had dropped from their often high, tensed position and were enjoying the fluidity.

The closeness Emilio felt to her transcended the merely physical. His spirit almost intermingled with hers as if they could dance until the end of time. *I am here. With her. I belong. For once I belong.* His desire for his body to be interwoven with hers felt natural—not forced or sexual—just the way of things. This was not the time for the poetry of words, for those missives in envelopes. He felt no need for Sabines to help him articulate his feelings because this sensation was beyond the words of the great master. It just was.

He didn't have to steal himself to feel emboldened, it just happened: he slid his right hand into her waiting one. The skin he had dreamt of touching so many times was coarser than he had anticipated, and the fingers so much stronger as he tried to interweave his tiny digits between hers.

She didn't react. She didn't even respond. She just allowed. *Has she worked out that the poem-sender is me. Has she been waiting for me to move beyond the page and become physical? Become real? Has she been anticipating, even inviting this connection?*

He squeezed her hand.

Her outline in the shadowed darkness turned to look down at him. He was aware she would not be able to see the love in his eyes or the gentle smile passing his lips, but she would discern his proud, diminutive stature and know it was him.

She squeezed his hand in return.

She squeezed his hand in return!

Emboldened, he made small circles with his index finger, caressing the soft pads at the base of her fingers. She replied by drawing a figure of eight in the centre of his palm. Or maybe it was the symbol of infinity?

He held his breath. *Please let this moment last forever.* Sighing. Audibly, but thankfully not loud enough for the cave to magnify into an echo.

Their fingers toyed with one other. Twirling, dancing, teasing. And then she rubbed her thumb upon his. And stopped. Her search found no digit to meet hers—merely a hardened, life-worn stump. Lillibet's hand froze, then dropped his like a puppeteer cutting the strings holding the marionette upright.

Emilio stood stock still. What had, moments ago, felt like the cave's cool retreat from the blazing sun, now felt like the frostiness of a morgue. He wanted to flee—to be away from this oppressive crowd, from this place. Away from Lillibet. *What just happened? She knows my right thumb was absent, everyone knows this. So why, when she* touched my *stump, did her tender responses stop so abruptly? What happened? I don't understand.* He hated his stump; it revolted him, as it had revolted her. He was useless. Unloveable.

'Hahahahahaha,' the group called out collectively as an unimaginative acoustic experiment.

'Hahahahahaha,' replied the cave.

And then a small miracle happened: Lillibet fumbled in the dark to relocate his hand. Once found, she enclosed it in hers. She squeezed more tightly than before. Then squeezed again. A rush of energy coursed his body like an electric shock.

'I love you,' called the crowd.

'I love you,' replied the cave.

*

The twins didn't fight that evening—not with mutual opponents nor each other. Emilio's stomach was too unsettled from the cave trip and the public must, always, be sheltered from the image of an ailing, vulnerable wrestler. And if one twin was out of action, both were. Whether they liked it or not, they came as a package. Consequently, being away from the main arena they were the last to hear of Lillibet's accident. It was the clashing soundwaves of the ambulance's siren that heralded harm. Emilio and Emiliano both rushed to their front caravan window. *What's happened? Who's been hurt?* The flashing blue lights cast an eerie glimpse of the crowd's anxious expressions as a stretcher was carried from the arena by two impossibly handsome paramedics. The twins both glimpsed the patient's peacock blue skirt billowing from the stretcher like a slowly deflating parachute trapping a blue sky inside its folds. Simultaneously jostling for the door, they crashed into each other. Then ran, four small feet kicking the dust of an arid summer. Both trained to access their energy supplies and convert them into explosive responses when needed—they ran. They ran towards their love.

Pilar, her flushed face barely containing her distress, held tight to Lillibet's right ankle anchoring her friend as if she might take off and float towards the heavens. The rest of the troupe spilled out of the arena in a visual rattle bag of capes, oiled flesh, and bowler hats. Their masks barely disguised the agitation their bodies were unable to conceal. One of their own had fallen.

'My leg!' she screamed. 'It's too much. Help me. Help me!' Lillibet writhed on the stretcher as a paramedic firmly placed an oxygen mask over her fevered face with practised pressure, hand on shoulder as he attempted to guide her back to a safe shore.

'Breathe my darling. Breathe slowly. That's it. Well done,' whispered Pilar.

The twins arrived at her side like primary school children crossing the sports day finish line. They were too pumped full of alarm to concern themselves with how their behaviour might appear to the gossips. Nor how they might appear to each other.

Emiliano ran to the left side of Lillibet's stretcher, seizing her hand with urgency. Passion was pumping from his heart to his fingertips and through them into hers. She felt a jolt of static.

At precisely the same moment, Emilio arrived at the right side of Lillibet's stretcher and tenderly took her other hand—protectiveness pumped from his heart into his fingertips and through them into hers. She felt a gentleness trickle up her right arm.

And that, combined with the agonies of a fractured femur, was rather a lot for one body to contain.

The troupe shied from the term 'post-mortem' after an incident. To invite the word 'death' into their ring, in whatever language, felt like playing with the gods. But whichever name they chose, they still needed to review the event. Not to attribute blame, for blame is insidious and eats away at trust, but to try to prevent any such thing happening again.

When the tale of that night was retold in years to come it was always described as 'just one of those things'. A freak accident. An error on Lillibet's part that could have happened to any wrestler in any match. An occupational risk. Lillibet's opponent, Scarlett Vixen, had, that night, executed a much-rehearsed throw. She had lifted Lillibet high on outstretched arms, bated the crowd with anticipation, and then thrown her in a swirl of plaits and petticoats into the ropes. Lillibet performed an oh so familiar move, bracing her body enough to ensure sufficient force would be generated to propel her back towards Scarlett Vixen, but not so rigid her body become a weapon. She fell onto the ropes, but their tautness spat her back and she bounced into the air. In the process her left foot somehow involuntarily hooked below one of the lower ropes. The tension jerked her body back and then propelled her limp rag doll form at a 45-degree angle onto the floor of the ring, landing on her side with the vulnerable leg beneath her. The referee skipped over on his tip toes and commenced the count: 10, 9,8. Lillibet didn't so much as scream, but released a howl. The crowd were relishing the drama: 4, 3. Scarlett Vixen knew this scenario was unrehearsed, could tell the difference between her opponent's cry for dramatic effect and the cry of a sentient being in pain. 2, 1: the referee slapped his palm onto the floor declaring the match had been both lost and won. Pushing a strand of his greased hair back into place, he grabbed Scarlett Vixen's hand ready to herald a victory salute. She, however, dodged out his way and fell on her knees next to the whimpering Lillibet.

Gently moving aside the plait laying across Lillibet's face, she knelt closer: 'It's okay, darling. It will all be okay.' She then turned to the referee with slow steady eyes and shouted: 'Get a bloody ambulance! Now!'

All future tellings recounted how the noise of the crowd rippled from a baying chant to a quiet murmur in less than a minute as the realisation that something had gone badly wrong took hold. Some parents quickly ushered children out of the arena while shielding their tender eyes. One woman burst into tears of shock as she realised of all the catastrophes she perpetually feared every day, one had come to pass.

The cry of 'First Aid! First Aid!' was passed from person to person until it arrived to disturb Ricardo's game of cards in the humidity of the men's changing rooms. As the wrestlers' own medic, he was not primed for action as he should have been. It took him somewhere between ten seconds and an eternity to compute that he was needed, now. By the time he had grasped his bag (which may as well have had the word 'Inadequate' printed on it due to its paltry array of used bandages and a few plasters) and ran into the ring, he had to prise apart the protective ring of wrestlers around Lillibet. Instinctively they had formed a tight huddle to maintain her dignity from the greedy gossiping eyes of the audience. Such a spectacle was a bonus beyond what their ticket price had guaranteed as the evening's entertainment: a melee of wrestlers, all still in costume but no longer in character, forming a human shield around one of their own.

Pilar was dashing between Lillibet's side and the entrance of the arena, willing the ambulance to arrive and transmitting the absence of news back to the patient with as much conviction as she could muster: 'It's on its way. It won't be long now.' Lillibet's pain was her pain too. It was at times like this she was acutely aware of how closely aligned they were. She was yet to develop the life skills to manage such empathy: distress ran rampant through her veins.

In contrast, Miguel had the experience borne of his longer years. He had consoled children with playground injuries, bee stings, allergic reactions, and night terrors. He had nursed elderly parents as they faced the frailty and finally their mortality. He had managed his own dark grief, the humiliation of bankruptcy, the pain of unrequited love. Logic kicked in to override all other emotions in a crisis, his calmness reassuring those less able to contain anxieties. He had learned to look ahead down a timeline to a point beyond when the initial drama had passed, and healing was underway. In among a troupe whose drama was their second nature, Miguel was needed. He sat beside Lillibet telling her to imitate his breathing, leading her out of a panic state into one that wasn't calm but was at least drawing more oxygen than nitrogen into her lungs.

The troupe stood back to make space for Ricardo. They later confessed to sharing the same unspoken thought— *Does he actually have any training? Why are we waiting for a crisis to ask this question?* as they watched him place a dry towel on her forehead. 'My leg! My leg!' she screamed. With his fingers pressed on the delicate skin on the inside of her wrist he took her pulse, or at least seemed to. 'My leggggg!'

When he produced a stethoscope from his bag and unravelled it like a waking octopus, Gabriel could bear the farce no more.

'I'm calling again to check why the ambulance is taking so long,' he announced with an unfamiliar authoritative air, and pushed his way out of the crowd in search of a phone. The collective sigh was audible—thankfully someone had taken charge. It was reassuring to feel that proper medical care may be nearby. It was also good not to have Gabriel in the centre of the group—no one is comfortable in the presence of a skeleton at the scene of an accident.

Ricardo was pushed aside as others stepped in. Armadillo shifted Lillibet onto her back, removed his cape, folded it, and put it tenderly under her head. Red Fox stroked Lillibet's arm, telling her that her leg didn't look so bad. Since childhood he had developed a skill for fluent lying.

Scarlett Vixen was in tears of shock and self-imposed guilt no level of vindication by others suppressed.

'It wasn't your fault.'

'These things can happen, it's the nature of our sport.'

'She'll be back in the ring in no time.'

Amidst this hullabaloo no one questioned the curiosity of the twins skidding up to Lillibet's stretcher. Except the twins, who later questioned not themselves but each other. As each focused 90% of their attention on Lillibet, they spent the remaining 10% of their focus on each other's actions and motives: *Why did he run out of the caravan without hesitation? Why did his impetus override caution about what others might witness? Why was his response disproportionate to concern for a fellow injured wrestler. What was going on between him and Lillibet?* Something had escaped from its box.

'My leggggg!' screamed Lillibet.

Six

Gabriel knew through gossip and rumour amongst the troupe if Lillibet had been demanding that day—little else was as occupying as passing judgement each on the other. She had been pushing herself too hard in training; she had shouted at Miguel; she had flounced out of her caravan for no reason. On such a day he would prepare a dinner of tortillas and beans, to serve Pilar once Lillibet had retired to bed. Like most men from his village accustomed to their mothers, sisters and wives providing sustenance, his cooking repertoire was limited. But the meals he made for Pilar were infused with care and love. At other times he took his beloved on walks across sand dunes or through shaded forests. Every morning he picked wildflowers and left them for her to find, wrapped in the back page of yesterday's newspaper and placed on the step of her caravan for when she opened the door to the new day.

After the first flourish of their courtship, Gabriel became self-conscious about public expressions of his feelings. He would rapidly round on himself and drop Pilar's hand, or remove the arm he had draped over her shoulder. He more than compensated in private when he played an attentive audience to Pilar, listening to childhood anecdotes or analysis of her increasing ambivalence towards Lillibet and their friendship. Never did she talk about ambitions for her future; still, she was a shadow of her famous friend.

Likewise, their lovemaking tempered from the first flush of passion when they explored each other's bodies to the smallest detail, like explorers delighting in new lands, to a more familiar frequent pattern that was tender and functional.

They rubbed along just fine, a happy harmony and companionship. Most of the single members of the troupe envied their quiet equilibrium. Most of the married members felt homesick for their spouses as they watched the lovers stroll with arms entwined. All that was fine, until Gabriel's wrestling career took a steep trajectory from a steady, low plateau to an impressive ascent. Initially he won the occasional round, but then as older wrestlers were becoming less agile, their lifestyle taking its toll, Gabriel conversely became nimbler. The public were increasingly asking: 'Who is the man inside the skeleton costume?' What is his character like? Is he single/eligible/desirable?" Gabriel was hot property.

The culture of celebrity had been imposed on the wrestling world. There was a degree of inevitability about this; their life was a heady cocktail of flamboyant sport, loyal audiences, and big prize money, these being the conditions on which celebrity culture flourishes. That and sex.

As the embodiment of strength and courage, vitality and fun, the luchadores were considered public property: the nation was proud of their homespun stars. And the masks! Their air of mystery, that feeling of the hidden and forbidden, was highly seductive.

Fantasies of all shapes and sizes, of every type of personality imaginable, were easily projected on the wrestlers by members of the public, driven by the pervasive media-driven culture. Gossip magazines feigned concern with headlines speculating about Red Fox's change in his marital relationship after winning so much money, or in faux concerns about Armadillo's mental health positioned alongside a photo of him flushed and sweaty while downing a tequila shot in a low-ceilinged, darkened bar.

Some of the troupe revelled in the attention, no matter how shallow.

They courted paparazzi, enjoyed the camera's flash, sold their privacy and that of their compatriots. They were easily seduced.

And, like human snowballs, the more they rolled in this pit of gossip and falsity, the more convinced they became of their importance, until the media machine morphed them into their own creation, rendering them unable to distinguish the parts of themselves that were true from the media-imposed fantasy.

Gabriel was at the centre of a virtuous cycle: the more his fanbase expanded, the more paparazzi jostled to capture shots of him they could sell to the highest bidder. The more his photo appeared in the celebrity magazines, the more his fanbase rose. And so the modern cycle of fame begetting fame reached a tipping point in which minimal fuel was required to increase its momentum.

It is said wealth begets wealth. It also begets envy. Gabriel wasn't naïve—he knew his time in the spotlight would be limited. Once he lost more than one match in a row, the fickle public's attentions would pivot onto the next rising star. So he should metaphorically make hay while the sun shone.

*

On the night after Lillibet's accident, Pilar declined Gabriel's invitation to join some others for drinks and an inevitable analysis of what had occurred. How had she fallen so badly? Was her career in jeopardy? On visiting her hospital bed earlier, Pilar had observed how Lillibet's mood had shifted from the initial shock, anger and frustration to a more mellow acceptance and willingness to give herself over to recovery. This allowed Pilar to relax her shoulders, elongate her neck and take deep breaths of relief. Reluctant to break this newfound peace, the last thing she desired was to frequent a cacophonous bar with a jangle of opinions, most seeking a hook on which to hang blame.

Gabriel, however, needed stimulus. And the attention he had gotten used to, that he craved. If Pilar wasn't willing to provide this, he was no longer prepared to sit quietly in her caravan, cooking and chatting—he wanted excitement. Pilar clearly wasn't going to meet his needs, but a crowded bar with the adoration of his fellow luchadores and the hungry public, would. If only, she thought, if only his ego would slow down and consider that some members of this public would be women— keen to associate with him, to garner his attentions. Women more than willing to fill the adoration vacuum her weary self was unable, at this time, to provide.

In the early evening, without reassurance or even kind words, Gabriel departed the company of this dear, careworn woman, and like a magpie, was compelled by the rustle of the shiny new, often dressed up in sequins and satin.

*

Emilio had, over the years become resigned to adult women treating him with fond but patronising maternalism. Somehow, they were unable to see the adult man trapped in a small body and oh so frequently he experienced being spoken to in simple vocabulary imparted in lilting tones—often with a slight head tilt.

It came as no surprise when the matron adopted this same demeanour. *Here we go again,* he thought. *There's no point getting annoyed. Suck it up.* Although not dislocated by the tedious familiarity of her tone, he was confused by her words.

'Back so soon! You really can't keep away, can you?'

He furrowed his brow. 'I'm here to visit Lillibet Garcia. She was brought here last night. Where might I find her?'

'Well, where you left her of course!' the matron mocked. 'We're not in the habit of moving our patients every five minutes. We're busy with the business of nursing in case you haven't noticed." With one hand she flicked loose fingers in the general direction of the end of the ward, resting her other hand gently atop his head. 'Now don't stay too long. Visiting hours finish at five. You've already tired her out enough for today.' She laughed, fondly.

As Emilio nodded greetings to the other female patients peering at him, bored in their beds, he made his way down the ward, his heart beating a loud rhythm in his ears, obstructing him from realising the obvious. Having spent all his life being mistaken for his brother, and vice versa, today he had somehow missed the clues.

Lillibet was propped regally in a cloud of white feathered pillows, her leg elevated above the starched hospital sheets. She looked quizzically at Emilio as he approached. 'Did you forget something?'

Not you as well, he thought. 'I'm Emilio, not Emiliano,' he clarified. 'I take it my brother has already paid you a visit?'

To give Lillibet her due, she was the mistress of social composure. 'Yes, he's just left, hence why I…'

He pressed his first finger to his pursed lips, determined not to allow his brother's shadow to intrude on this rare moment alone with her. He quickly altered his state by springing onto the bed, nesting his bottom next to her broken leg. 'Ouch, be careful!' she exclaimed as the bed vibrated on its castors, just enough to set a shudder in motion.

'I'm sorry,' he said with a pout, wondering to himself why he'd turned into some form of exaggerated mime artist. 'How is the leg? Are you in pain? Do you need anything?'

'I need to know when I'll be able to wrestle again.'

'What has the doctor said?'

'Oh, that one, she's pessimistic by nature. She said I won't be back in the ring for at least a year, but I'm sure…'

She was unable to finish her sentence for large, pregnant tears cascaded down her lovely cheeks. Initially they were droplets but then gathered volume and speed to rapidly become a torrent. Emilio sat, taking her hand in his, for once not feeling self-conscious. He held her hand.

He held her soul. And she surrendered to the release of accumulated emotions, knowing this kind soul would catch her. She connected with the pain in her femur. She connected with the disorientation of being so far from home. She connected with her shame at having treated the kind, loyal Pilar so meanly. She connected with the gratitude for Miguel's unswerving support. She connected with the longing for Consuelo to be there to give her maternal healing. And she connected with the softness in her spirit Emilio's poems evoked.

And between sobs she choked out, 'I just want to go home.'

Emilio nodded, slowly. He so often longed for the familiar smells of Maria's kitchen, to taste her cooking, and to feel the squeeze of her hand on his shoulder. But Lillibet's home and his home were in different lands and for each to return would be to put mountain ranges and borders between them. That was unbearable to him—now or ever.

'I know, I know,' he soothed. 'But for now you are here, and you'll remain at least until your leg is out of plaster and you can board a plane.'

She nodded and sobbed some more.

'What would help, my love? How can I make it more bearable for you here and now?' he whispered, keeping his gaze on her downcast eyes.

'You're doing it.' She squeezed his hand and turned her bloodshot eyes and puffy tear-streaked face towards him. And he saw the most beautiful woman in the world.

Emilio already knew that he would wrap this moment in tissue paper and store it in his memory bank forever. It was like a butterfly that lands as a whisper, catches the breeze and is gone, yet in its delicacy leaves an imprint, invisible to the eye but lingering in the heart.

The matron in her brusque manner broke the beauty of the moment by impatiently announcing the end of visiting time. Emilio scooped up the visit though, and as a mother keeps her baby's first hair curl safely in a locket, he held tight to the energy of their connected hands and hearts.

'I promise I will come back tomorrow,' he told Lillibet as her heavy eyelids settled and she nodded him goodbye with a gentle smile.

The tenderness of the mood stayed with him for most of his bus journey home. For once he wasn't irritated by the stares of strangers fascinated as if they had never seen a person such as he before. If only they knew there was an identical version roaming at large! He managed to secure a seat and today decided not to relinquish it despite the passive aggressive mutterings of a fellow passenger who informed anyone willing to grant him an audience that in his view, his oh so important view, 'children' should not occupy seats when adults stood. Emilio merely leant back against the stickiness of the plastic seat that retained the heat of the long day's ferocious sun and replied silently while resolutely staring ahead: *I am not a child. I am an adult man. I am not a child. I am a man in love. I am not a child. I know a beautiful woman who might just be falling in love with me in return.*

Glancing around the bus as it rattled down the potholed road, he smiled in the knowledge of how rich his life felt compared with these mean people around him. He may not have a tall body, but he had a heart full of love, something they might never know.

His thoughts drifted from the discomfort of the journey back to the hospital. Behind the sweet memory of those precious moments with Lillibet he recalled the matron's confusion on mistaking him for his brother. It wasn't the first time in his life this had happened and undoubtedly it wouldn't be the last. Yet today felt more significant: *why had Emiliano been at Lillibet's bedside?* His mind jolted with the recollection of yesterday, running from their caravan to Lillibet's side as she was carried into the ambulance like a fragile flower. Emiliano was there too, taking Lillibet's left hand as he had taken her right; it had been like looking into a mirror, seeing not only a somatic reflection but his own unguarded emotions: panic, concern, tenderness, attentiveness. It was as if every emotion he had careered through in the last 24 hours had been experienced twice. Was he narcissistically projecting onto his twin, or was there an ominous shadow looming over his recently found brightness?

*

It wasn't such a bad thing for Lillibet to be incapacitated. Her physical pain, the precarity this injury placed on her wrestling career—her life's passion, her identity and her source of income—were all in jeopardy. Conversely, the benefit was the brake it put on the hurtling pace of her life and the creation of the opportunity for her to just stop and reflect. By sitting immobile in her hospital bed, she could gather a sense of perspective, processing her thoughts and emotions about her crazy, meteoric rise to stardom, could see more clearly how she had been feted by the press and placed upon a pedestal as a role model for young women across the towns and villages of her country. A weighty responsibility to carry.

It came as a relief to just lie for a while and gather herself. Her removal from her daily life into this place of care and recovery felt cathartic. Reflections flooded in: *I so hate the overused metaphor of a journey, people overuse it to describe life's shifts and turns, yet I sort of feel my emotions are travelling from one place to another. Is this what people mean by 'cathartic'? Am I leaving my old self or am I connecting to who I am deep inside? It's confusing, confusing but okay.* In this bed she was forced to listen not only to her own thoughts but those of others as, for the time, she was trapped.

Pilar consumed the whole of the next day's visiting hours, much to matron's palpable irritation. The latter believed her patients should rest up and recover quietly with minimum fuss. They certainly shouldn't play host to the variety of loud, emotional characters who Lillibet warmly welcomed day after day. During Pilar's visit, the matron made a point of frequently walking past the end of Lillibet's bed and audibly tutting her disapproval. This was, however, to no effect, as her tuts were drowned by Pilar's sobs.

In a role reversal, Lillibet was subjected to the outpouring of a semi-coherent stream of words from her friend who was sitting on the side of the bed. *What? How? But, but… If only… I don't believe this. What if? Why, why, why. Is it me? Is it him?* Her weight pulled the starched sheets tight across Lillibet's thighs as she gestured wildly, uncharacteristically venting about her beloved Skeleton.

Had he changed?

Had she just gotten to know the real him?

Why was his behaviour so erratic?
Had she changed?
Had she done something wrong?
Was he under some form of stress?
Had he fallen out of love with her?
Was she, deep down, just unattractive?
Had she unwittingly upset him?
Had he received bad news from home he was unable to share?
Did he prefer the company of his mates?
Was she being too demanding?
Was she not demanding enough?

Lillibet didn't even attempt to answer. She merely lay still watching the unstable rattling ceiling fan, allowing her friend to empty herself of her anxieties and insecurities. And she bided her time, waiting for the inevitable question, Pilar was finally no longer able to continue dancing around. 'Lillibet—do you think he has met someone else?'

'Yes,' replied the patient.

'Do you think…' Pilar halted mid-question on hearing her friend's reply. 'Yes! You say yes! Yes! But why would you say that?'

Lillibet knew sometimes true friendship demands brutal honesty, even if it may feel unkind. She inhaled a deep preparatory breath, 'Because his behaviour suggests his attention's elsewhere, with someone else.'

Lillibet couldn't look at Pilar. She was unable to bear the hurt. Pilar gulped a sob. She attempted to swallow it again but as it hit her gut it exploded back up into her throat and escaped her mouth. 'How can you be so cruel?'

'Darling, I'm your best friend. I'm not being cruel. I'm

just trying to protect you from your own tender heart. He's being inattentive, when once he showered you with affection. He no longer spends his spare time with you when once he just couldn't get enough. His mind is elsewhere. His balls probably are too.'

On realising Pilar's sob was likely to gather momentum into a torrent loud enough to disturb the ward, Lillibet decided to call a halt to imparting more home truths.

'He's just not worth you my darling. You deserve so much more.' She folded Pilar's fragile, bony hand into the comfort of her stronger one with a protective squeeze.

Lillibet had intended to speak to Pilar today about the twins, having reached the realisation she could no longer deny that both Emilio and Emiliano had fallen in love with her. A heat rose in her solar plexus when she thought of them—one so kind and tender and the other so much fun. But there was obviously no love lost between the brothers. It was an imperfect, jagged triangle. It was too much of a distraction. *Keep focused*, she told herself, *you can't afford such emotions, not if you're going to get strong again, get back in that ring and fight. Focus.*

She spent hours trying to distract herself, immersing her thoughts in a book. When that didn't work, she downgraded to magazines. But her concentration was as fragile as morning frost on feathers. She had tried listening to radio programmes full of faux joviality, but her mind wandered to the voice in her head that constantly debated itself like chattering chipmunks—what was going to happen next between them? Were her emotions wrong, forbidden?

The nurses shrugged off her requests to provide her

crutches so she could force her body to override her mind and distract herself with physical movement. It seemed the doctor had ordered rest, and the doctor's orders were to be obeyed.

Her body felt heavy on the bed. She longed to fly, to escape these thoughts; a complex web of emotions had already woven tightly between herself and the twins, for she feared how, when translated to action, they may play out in ways that lead to heartbreak for herself, for all three of them even. No, this was no good, she would not allow this to run away with her.

The matron walked over to Lillibet's bed with a weariness when she called. Not more requests from her most demanding patient, surely?

'If the diminutive wrestlers visit again, either together or alone, please tell them I don't want to see them—either of them. Tell them to leave me alone.' Her voice quavered as she scrunched a beautiful manilla paper in her palm.

'With the greatest of pleasure,' assured matron, delighted to finally have a degree of order restored to her ward.

*

Emilio didn't so much as have possession of it, rather it had possession of him. Fear. He knew that like love, fear is not a singular emotion; rather it is a composite of undefinable shards like a kaleidoscope fractures and reforms according to who holds it. But now it felt like being stuck in an unending dark tunnel.

He was gripped by it as if he were the protagonist of a horror film, trapped in the ubiquitous dark cellar in an isolated, decaying house that rattled like timber and wattle in a storm. He was paralysed by fear, so afraid of loss he was unable to be still in mind or body. This restlessness compelled him, in the middle of the night, to walk, fast-paced, round and round the wrestling ring, ducking under the bottom rope and planting his feet firmly on the sprung floor. He walked clockwise as if this might wind the night forward into a new dawn when everything would be resolved. After a while he stopped, turned and reversed his steps, increasing his anticlockwise pace as if unwinding time's spool, drawing him back to his moment of bliss—when he was seated on Lillibet's hospital bed, their hands clasped together as tightly as an oyster shell.

He feared loss.

The morning light started to permeate the heavy fabric of the tented auditorium. Exhausted and sweaty, but still without the containment of his spiralling emotions, Emilio slumped.

Laying on his back atop the mandala-painted centre of the ring, wide-eyed staring at the canvas ceiling, he shouted, 'I don't want to lose her. I can't lose her.' And then in a whisper, fearful of malicious gods: 'Not to him. Especially not to him.'

*

Emiliano waded through anxious dreams in which he, as always in his dreamscape, was the protagonist. Tonight, however, his subconscious had not cast him as the swashbuckling hero hacking through forests: instead he was a small man, shrinking at an alarming rate, becoming smaller. He was accompanied by a goddess with long, dark silken hair laid out on a white pillow as she reclined on crisp bedsheets attired in a purple satin robe. His avatar was invisible to this goddess; he shouted to her in futile attempts to attract her attention, but his voice emerged muffled as if underwater. Standing to her right side, the gaze of her deep shining eyes was firmly directed away from him, towards her left. And there, in that spot stood his mirror image: a body resembling his precisely but not him. His goddess smiled beatifically at this other self, her face lit with the radiance of the sun. In the bathed light of this warmth, the mirror image grew, expanding, filling the space around his body with an orange aura. He called out again with a sound that strangled itself in his throat, deeper and further submerged, where the light couldn't find it.

He woke with a gasping jolt, gripping his bedsheet tightly with both hands. And the tormenting realisation ran deep through his subconscious, an excruciating fear of loss.

Seven

London had afforded Josefina a freedom typical of the first sweet taste of anonymity a large city provides a girl who has escaped small town claustrophobia. The fast pace of life suited her, and she loved being swept on the river-flow of human bodies in currents of the underground system, along the timeless streets. She revelled in the sensory privilege of watching a film on its day of release projected onto a giant screen with a multi-amplified soundtrack; or standing at the shining metal bar of an Italian coffee shop late at night, drinking bitter coffee in the company of beautiful young gay men. She loved it all. Most of all she loved the variety of lovers the city provided, purely for her pleasure.

The absence of anyone to scorn or reprimand her meant she could enthusiastically assume a lifestyle that, if known to them, would mortify her conventional parents. This city was so far removed from her parents' orbit—geographically, culturally, and morally. Liberation came to Josefina in the form of being free from the stream of her mother's endless prying questions about stuff and nonsense, as well as from her father's infinite unsought advice about how she should dress/speak/behave to secure herself a good husband, this imaginary man who apparently had to pay no heed to how he dressed/spoke/

behaved to secure her as his bride.

Alas it didn't take long in indulging in this lifestyle before Josefina's father's carefully allocated allowance ran out. The city was fun but that came with a hefty financial cost—the money trickled through her fingers at an alarming rate. It was, she realised, time for her to downgrade from her central hotel with a concierge and wonderful treetop view over Hyde Park, to something more befitting her new role as an independent, self-reliant woman-something more bijou.

Some may have called it a bedsit, she preferred to use the agent's term of 'studio apartment', with the attendant connotation of an artistic lifestyle. She relished the fanciful idea of becoming a painter or model in this studio, a muti functional space where she also invited her fleeting lovers who were more interested in the curve of her hips than in the square footage of her living space. It was a room with endless possibility.

The rent for this compact space consumed almost half of the meagre salary she earned from the administrative jobs she was undertaking. With little ambition to find work, which was either more taxing or more permanent, but with the freedom which accompanies the absence of dependents, the remaining money of her monthly pay was hers. Dresses, makeup, and socialising all within her financial reach. Her one stipulation to herself was to allocate a small sum each month with which to purchase books. Perusing bookshops stacked high with choice, feeling the weight of her purchases in her hands, inhaling the smell of the printed pages before dashing home to consume them under her bed covers beside a single bar electric heater, also fell into her 'having a good time' category. She wasn't solely about bars and chatting to men in late night chip shop queues; she craved stimulus for her mind as well as for her senses.

Her father's weekly letters instructed her, in an increasingly clipped tone, to return 'home' and apply herself to the dual tasks of settling down and making the most of her education, which, having funded her education, he viewed as his own investment. In turn, Josefina tried to resist a deeply ingrained guilt inherent in her Catholic upbringing, knowing inevitably it would, with a magnetic force, draw her back. But for now, this little studio and these rainy streets were home.

Being in possession of a creative mind, a diverse and vibrant imagination, she could have easily become depleted by the grind of her administrative job. Filing, taking notes, completing budget sheets was not what she had been created for. To tolerate the tedium was, however, a means to an end: the means being a regular, reliable income, and the ends being the fun to be had by a young single woman with a recently discovered appetite for pleasure.

*

If Josefina's lovers could be classified into a type, it wasn't about height, hair colour, dress sense, humour, race, or education: rather it was their common desire to not develop attachments. Some were married, some single, some divorced. None sought commitment. In this respect, each was highly compatible with Josefina. She enjoyed the transience of these relationships—they provided her a sense of liberation. Living in a city that was not pulling her down into the weightiness of convention went hand in glove with flitting her way through temporary but passionate encounters. For the first time in her life she was in control of her money, time, and body.

She was conscious of the liminality of her state—hovering between university studies and a future path of either career or marriage. She fully intended to drop into this space, at least temporarily. Liminality bought liberation. Most of all, she enjoyed wasting time: beyond her father's supervision she was no longer obliged to commit to pursuing some form of deferred gratification, but instead could enjoy the present for what it was—a gift.

It took another decade for Josefina to become fully aware that while at the time she had viewed this period as time out, she was in fact accumulating techniques for future deployment. She did, in short, refine the skills of seduction. Such skills can come in useful during economic collapse when resourcefulness and resilience are critical, especially when she found herself in danger of living on the margins.

When economies crash the impact is never universal; those who began the epoch with the most money, the most property, the most connections, invariably emerge from the chaos (once the financial dust has settled) with more. On the other hand, those for whom security was already precarious can easily be pushed over a precipice. When the economic collapse of her country arrived like an uninvited guest, Josefina firmly belonged to the latter group.

After the glorious two and a half London years Josefina finally succumbed to her parents' unrelenting pressure and boarded a plane to return to a place she no longer considered home. But what could she do next? Where would she find a direction? The sands of time of her twenties now slipping through her hands predictably heralded the onset of her depression: finding herself yet again unstretched teaching English in an ad hoc way to unmotivated students, constrained in her social life by the expectations of both her family and society. She began to own the disappointment others projected on her. It was a small step for her to revert to her previous persona of petulant teenager with monosyllabic grunts, amplified by an overwhelming sense her parents didn't like her. Most days she didn't like herself.

To stem the momentum of a downward spiral she reached out to old friends, those from school and university with whom the connective tissue had, of late, become thinly stretched. Josefina was aware she had neglected to feed and nurture these bonds while away, ignoring letters and the occasional phone call. So immersed had she been in her London life she'd failed to notice the withering of these friendships until she needed the warmth rooted in long-term familiarity.

When the occasional friend did concede to meet her, the chasm between them was evident without either needing to acknowledge it. They would update her with news of their weddings, pregnancies, children, careers, houses, and days mapped out with routines built on aspirations. Josefina became increasingly conscious that tales of a life in a faraway city, a dead-end job and the delights of multiple lovers wouldn't portray her as the sort of friend who could blend fluidly with their social circles. But what else could she share? Her tribe had reformed and regrouped with invisible but hard edges that no longer had the elasticity to accept her for who she now was.

Her only option, she felt, was to embark on shapeshifting into the person she believed they wanted her to be—a woman who wouldn't be perceived as a threat to their humourless lives, their fractious marriages or the moral upbringing of their children. She made herself smaller.

Consequently, her inclusion in the list of dinner party invitees noticeably shifted. Often, she found herself seated next to bachelors her friends' husbands knew, around a table abundant with shining silver cutlery and dull conversation. Two days later she would decline the predictable invite to a date sent by a boring single man, which in turn provoked a quizzical phone call from her friend extolling the merits of said man, pointing out that he was single/solvent/without a criminal record and she 'really isn't in a position to be so choosy.'

Dinner party invitations soon became spaced out from fortnightly to monthly, presumably due to the diminishing pool of available single men and the fact that to invite her solo would seriously disrupt their alternate man/woman/man/woman seating plan. Her very presence would disrupt their conventionality.

Best to give it all one last go, she thought, when an invitation on a stiff cream card slipped through her letterbox. Best see if she could fit in.

'Tell me, how long have you known the Sanchezs?' politely enquired the single, solvent, without-a-criminal-record man seated to her right around this dinner table laid in tessellating patterns of polished cutlery and cut glass.

Josefina tried not to fidget but the collar of her dress was gripping her neck like a claw.

'Since high school. Myself and Valeria were in the same class. And you?'

'I only met Valeria at their engagement party. I was at university with Dario—we both studied engineering. After that I moved to Venezuela for a job at a refinery for nearly five years. I kept getting promotions so I stayed longer than I initially intended. I only moved back here three months ago. When you reach my professional level you have to wait a while for a suitable job—they're few and far between. I had hoped to make deputy director by now, but I'm confident I can shift up to that within the next eighteen months.'

Josefina refolded her napkin awaiting the 'And what about you, what's your line of work?' question typical of such a humdrum conversational flow, but it never arrived. Instead, this man continued to transmit.

'I don't have much spare time due to work pressures, but I do prioritise keeping myself fit. I'm a good 10k runner. I try to do three a week, usually before sunrise when few people are up. I believe a disciplined body shows a disciplined mind.'

She considered sticking the prongs of one of the silver forks into the back of her hand to check she was still alive, nodding and muttering 'Absolutely' exactly as expected from a dutiful audience.

*

The agreement amongst hostesses was that Josefina's

'performance' at these dinner parties was lacking. Where they had expected demureness, combined with gratitude and mixed with wit, Josefina had delivered sarcasm with a touch of belligerence, albeit while looking stunning and radiant. It was difficult to pinpoint the recipe for her allure, but somehow her presence at the dinner party table felt like a threat to the status quo. The following day after such an evening, the hostesses often found themselves making salon appointments for a new, sharper hair style, or in boutique changing rooms trying on jeans much tighter fitting than they had ever worn before. They found themselves casting glances at their husbands, to detect if they were, like moths, being drawn to the flame. What their insecurities failed to recognise was that Josefina would rather stick hot pokers in her eyes that adopt their dull lifestyles with their duller husbands. She was willing to make herself a little smaller to fit in, but not that small!

Josefina had a worrying sense her minor attempts to blend in with the biegeness had shrunken her brain, or rather her critical thinking processes. She had taken to reading the gossip magazines, initially just at the hairdressers where she could scan pictures of the photoshoots while listening to the conversations of her fellow customers in their various states of hairdressing disarray. The celebrity circus grew at a greater speed than her hair, however, and she consequently found herself a month or so out of date in conversations with the hostesses—her knowledge of which stranger in the public eye was pregnant/getting married/losing weight/gaining weight tended to be sorely lacking. Her only solution was to start buying the magazines herself.

To be spending some of her income on this trivia felt

like a betrayal to her own intelligence. Yet she found that between editions, her mind would drift to wondering about the lives of celebrities she would never meet, and probably would never, in reality, get along with. She became eager to discover how their lives were unfolding— initially in a casual, throwaway way, but over a period of weeks in a more consuming, distracting manner until there was less and less space in her head for thoughts about literature, architecture, and films. She even found herself experiencing the emotions of shock and grief when a film star died in a freak accident. She had been dumbed down, sucked into a vortex of triviality.

Her brain had become so full of mush that one rainy Monday in April she failed to join the dots when three of her private pupils all finished with the same sentence.

'I'm sorry Josefina. You know I love your lessons, but times being as they are I can no longer afford them. So next week will have to be my last lesson I'm afraid. I'm so sorry but I'm sure you understand.'

Was the sudden withdrawal from three unrelated students a curious coincidence? Had she been paying more attention she would have realised there is no such thing as coincidence.

Had she been paying attention she would have noticed that the price of tomatoes on every single market stall had doubled in the last month.

Had she kept hold of her little green car she would have noticed fuel prices shifting faster than a taxi metre.

When she did start noticing, the signs were everywhere. How could she have become so unaware? Every third day there were queues at the petrol station as drivers attempted to fill their tanks quickly, before the next price rise took hold. Each rise brought in its wake a subsequent increase in bus fares. More and more folks raced to sell their cars before the deluged market ensured more supply than demand, bringing the inevitable plummet in value typical of the free market.

Passenger numbers on buses declined quite rapidly as fewer and fewer people had jobs to travel to: unemployment figures danced in unison with the numbers of businesses filing for bankruptcy. Everything was connected.

The tangible signs of recession were, however, less disconcerting than the change in the national mood. Anxiety ran rife through the population, contagious yet invisible. And when two more of Josefina's students gave her notice on their lessons, she too began to catch it.

*

Josefina had detected not only a change in the mood of the population but a hint of autumn crispness which arrived without warning. She chose a seat under the faded café awning, half in, half out of the diminishing sun's rays and drew her scarf more tightly around her neck. The change was more than seasonal. Josefina's mindset was also shifting: if she continued living on borrowed time, she thought, refusing to acknowledge plummeting economics, then soon she would be living on borrowed money too.

Taking her old school calculator out of her bag, she set about revising her income and expenditure equation which had ticked along smoothly for so long. With two columns drawn up in her notebook it was undeniable that one side was increasing while the other was decreasing. Both at rapid paces. The calculator keys made a mocking rackety sound as her manicured nails tapped the figures in once, twice, three times—they failed to shift. It was evident that if she were to lose just one more student, she would be at risk of not being able to make the rent next month. Her mind went on a tour of her apartment, a meandering reflection full of fondness and anticipatory regret should she lose it. She danced her fingertips across the kitchen counter, tidied her scattered pile of magazines, and approved her choice of stainless-steel implements and blue glass drinking goblets. She plumped the cushions on her faded turquoise sofa. The springs long since collapsed, she now reserved sitting there for late evenings when from that position she could see the moon through the high window. The bedroom was her sanctuary from the world, where she could either be alone with her books or enjoy the pleasure of lovers. The tour ended in her mind as she left via the front door, turned the key securely in the lock and walked away from that place, that worn and somewhat tatty place which to her was home.

*

Josefina's Saturday mornings were free time. They used to be a popular slot for aspiring businesspeople to employ her in pursuit of improving their English as a vehicle to a correlated improvement in finances, and status. For the previous three weeks, these back-to-back lessons had been replaced with long, lingering trips to her local coffee shop. She knew she could no longer afford such indulgences, but somehow, she needed to retain a sense of pleasure amidst a swirling mood music of anxiety. These brief mornings of respite allowed her to relish watching people going about their business indulging her appetite for pastries, strong black coffee and flirting with the waiters.

She was aware she cut an attractive, slightly mysterious figure, sitting at a table alone. Her London habits were not so long behind her after all. Wearing a purple linen dress that rode up to her mid-thigh when she was seated, Josefina found it easy to command the waiter's attention—she merely had to cross and uncross her legs in a seated dance while casting her gaze down in mock demureness.

'Another coffee? Maybe another fresh pastry?' The waiter smiled. Had she detected a brief wink?

'Do you think I should?' she replied, stroking the handle of her coffee cup.

'Of course. What are Saturday mornings for if not to indulge yourself a little?'

She noted his hirsute eyebrows as he raised them into a question mark. She associated thick eyebrows with a strong libido, an association she knew was based purely on her research and unfounded in scientific evidence. While he skirted between the tables to instruct the barista to circle the milk on the top of her coffee into a heart shape, Josefina pulled out her notebook from her handbag. Rummaging, she located a pen and tucked it between her lipstick, keys and well-laundered handkerchief, a longtime gift from her late grandmother.

'One cappuccino,' flourished the waiter. He proudly placed it in front of her, the milk shifting to convey a curious cinnamon image of a pulsing heart. The schmaltziness made her wince and she felt a twitch in her left shoulder, but decided to proceed as planned.

'I seem to have forgotten my pen. I don't suppose you could lend me one?'

He pulled a pencil from behind his ear, noted it's rather sad, chewed end, and tucked it back in place.

'One moment, I'll fetch one for you.'

Ignoring sighs from other customers attempting to place orders, he hurried back to the bar in search of a pen suitable for the lady in purple. Josefina meanwhile appreciated the tightness of his trousers enhancing his neat bottom, but knew, as always, her interest was waning as soon as the thrill of the chase was over, and her prey had been captured.

She stirred her coffee, the heart shape turning into a spiral swirl, wishing she could concentrate on the urgent task in hand of sorting out her finances rather than being distracted by the waiter, the dance, the pen. Her wait was thankfully and predictably short as he promptly reappeared at her shoulder.

'Here you are. And I've checked it's working well.' Along with the pen he passed her a folded piece of yellow paper with jagged edges, typical of sheets torn hastily from a notebook. Experience told her without opening it that inside would be his name and phone number. This prey was way too easy to be satisfying.

Focus girl, she said to herself. *You're here for a purpose and that isn't collecting men's numbers.* Josefina once again took her notebook out of her bag, opened it on a virgin page and wrote the title 'Plan to balance finances' at the top. The blankness felt like a mirror to her mind.

In previous times, when business had been good, her rent had consumed one third of her monthly income.

With her depleted income it was greedily eating up half, an ever-growing child in need of more and more nourishment. The word 'rent' was small, four letters, one syllable. Yet it signified so much—it was her independence, her escape from the claustrophobia of her parent's apartment. She thought of the joyful weekends she had spent up ladders covering the tobacco-stained walls left by her predecessor with paint in shades of pink and lime green. The space she had created was vibrant with velvet cushions, woven rugs, cacti, and trailing houseplants. The space was hers.

Years ago two boyfriends who passed through her life in quick succession had each suggested they move in with her. Into her sacred space. She declined. Both. The idea of sharing horrified her. She had no desire to have the soft femininity compromised with clumsy male garments and odours. She relished consuming interior design magazines, fantasising about a more creative career in which she could play out her ideas at the financial expense of perfect couples with well-groomed, biddable children.

'Another coffee madam?' interrupted he of the tight trousers. As she jolted back into the brightness of the day, she noticed the waiter looking down at her notepad with its title above the page devoid of ideas. He saw such pages in the notebooks of customers on an almost daily basis, sometimes with the same vacuum of plans, sometimes with far too many furious crossings outs.

'Have the next coffee on me. And do please call me Sebastian,' he said in a hushed tone.

'It's fine, I can pay my own way," she said brusquely, snapping the notebook shut. The waiter's eyebrows raised.

A wave of vulnerability washed over her like a shadow

passing in front of the sun. 'You won't owe me anything,' he assured, his previous flirtatiousness replaced with a soft kindness.

'Okay,' she said. 'Thank you.' Josefina knew from this point she was going to have to choose between deviousness or graciousness if she were to survive this economic tidal wave with her independence intact. She chose graciousness. For now.

*

When both local and national journalists got wind of Armadillo, one of the greatest stars of Lucha Libre, having been found half-naked in a hotel room, attempting to retrieve any shred of dignity left to him, claiming to have been seduced, drugged, and robbed, it was as if the reporters' headlines wrote themselves. The coalescence of money, scandal, celebrity, and crime made them rub their hands with glee.

'ARMADILLO'S SEX AND DRUGS HELL' screamed the morning papers atop a photo of the victim displaying his bare, well-oiled torso. A photo admittedly taken in his glory days in the ring rather than in the three-star backstreet hotel room he'd woken in one torpid Sunday afternoon.

Memories had filtered into his consciousness in fragments with jagged edges until there were enough for him to piece together the chain of events into coherence. Embarrassing but coherent.

*

Emotions had been heightened at the Saturday evening fight. Lucha Libre was back in town. Locals had cobbled what few pesos they could find, donned their shiny masks and for that one evening suspended worries about money and jobs and families and their uncertain futures, and headed into the magical interwoven world of sport and carnivals that beckoned forth to deliver delicious escape.

Armadillo usually thrived when the troupe were on the road. As Julia, his wife, liked to announce publicly whenever the opportunity arose, her husband preferred his wrestling family to his blood family. Cousins, aunts, uncles, nephews, and his sister would laugh awkwardly, aware said husband's face was flushing a telling shade of red, as he looked closely at his feet and avoided a reply which should have been filled with utterances of rebuttal and reassurance.

Of late, things hadn't been right. If pushed to be more precise, Armadillo would have struggled. It was a sensation rather than a thought. To catch such a feeling makes it lose its essence, like pinning a butterfly in a jam jar until the movement of its wings declines to a whisper. He was not given to pondering, preferring to look ahead. Time and experience were linear: his life had been shaped by events moving in sequence, from school to his wrestling training. Hard graft brought success—there was a direct correlation between effort and reward. Likewise, the path to his marriage was textbook—he met Julia in his early twenties, they fell in love. A proposal, an engagement, seemed inevitable. Nevertheless, of late he found himself unable to drop instantaneously into the deep restful sleep he always relished without thought or gratitude.

The first arrival in Taxco had seen several of the troupe embarking on a sortie round the late-night market. Armadillo had gladly joined.

'Look at the budgies,' called Emilio to him, pointing upwards to the cages displaying the trapped, depressed birds, unitedly pecking in cacophony rather than chorus. Armadillo poked the bars of one cage with a stubby finger and enjoyed the strange sensation of the tiny creature pecking his flesh. Although the glass roof of the market was held high by steel girders, he still felt claustrophobia, trapped. The usual crowd of locals had gathered around them this evening, but now he felt that given a small amount of encouragement they would also peck at his flesh. He focused his attention on the pyramids of fruit at a corner stall, the orange flesh of papayas nestling in contrast to the jade hue of the custard apples, complemented by the prickly pears.

The market merchants felt privileged when a passing luchadore stopped to pay attention and admire their fruits, as if it were a personal blessing on their peaches. Armadillo squeezed a couple of avocados and selected the one closest to the threshold of ripeness. He held it out to the sweaty man by the cash till, who, like a mime artist, made hand gestures conveying the universal meaning of 'Please take it. I don't want to take your money. It's yours. You're very welcome. Enjoy.'

The lusciousness Armadillo usually enjoyed in such markets was somehow absent. There were still fruit and vegetables, nuts, seeds. herbs, and flowers all contributing to a general abundance, but the edges were frayed. Oranges had dimples bigger than moon craters, bananas had black imprints like inked fingerprints, and flowers wilted like jilted lovers, hanging their heads in shame.

He wasn't a naive man; he read the newspapers and listened to radio stations. Information about the rapid economic decline was omnipresent until the words 'depression' and 'poverty' were so inextricably linked it was impossible to separate cause and effect.

Was there a strong anxiety in the air did he imagine it? It had a cold, metallic tang that made him long for a mouthful of clear, fresh water. A burly stall holder offered him a fresh coconut, its top scalped off and a pink plastic straw bobbing foolishly in the juice. It sat cupped in his large hand with a comforting weight. Searching deep into his trouser pockets he found some odd pestos to toss to the skinny local kids. His hopes of this gesture abating their grinding, shrieking cries were short lived: the sight of these tarnished coins was like a magnet, drawing an ever-increasing group of raggedy children. Some were brave enough to touch the clothes, legs and hands of the wrestler and then flee, squealing, as in turn they received his mawkish growls and scowls like a pantomime villain.

The troupe changed the energy of a town as they paraded. They embodied fun, strength, and excitement. Armadillo felt grateful he wasn't a resident of this town as he imagined the deflation that would seep in after their departure—that which the locals had anticipated so long would have arrived and then passed in a blink. It would be nice to think his ego was misguided, and the townsfolk moved on to a new distraction, but sadly this was not the case: the wrestlers were a breath of fresh air, so needed in challenging times.

*

Limbering up kicked in early that evening, each wrestler flexing and stretching muscle and sinew until the tendons were visible under the skin like train tracks across a desert. Armadillo selected his most vibrant costume, green shorts the colour of jasmine after the rain, silver boots laced to his knees, all topped with a majestic red cape evoking the glory of the matador. He oiled his waxed chest, caressing the steroid-plumped expanses like a new lover. He was ready to entertain his public. Bring it on!

After the match, a heady cocktail of adrenaline, cortisol and testosterone ran through his bloodstream. His heart, pumping so loudly, made him believe it was audible to those in the adjacent room. He was virility in human form. And then came, with horrible predictability, like Monday mornings follow Sunday nights, the sensation he most hated—the payback when his body had to return the energy it had borrowed. If it were possible to pay good money to avoid this, he would willingly. As a compromise this evening, he paid a not insignificant amount of the winnings he had pocketed to the bartender: his only means of stretching his glory to its edge was through alcohol,

'Another round my friend,' Armadillo slurred, 'and an extra shot of tequila for me please.'

The bartender flashed him a sceptical look but knew better than to question such a readily paying customer. As the luchadore removed a roll of notes from his trouser pocket, it dislodged another. Gabriel intervened, one tequila closer to soberness than his friend, catching the money before it fell to the floor.

'Hold tight to this buddy. Do you want me to take care of it until tomorrow? Hang onto it for safekeeping?'

This offer from a place of kindness was met with a flash of gold-capped teeth, half-smile, half-grimace. 'Nah. I am the victor tonight. I can look after my winnings. If someone accosted you in a dark alley they could blow you and your skinny bones over with one breath. But me—it would need ten men to get this money off me.'

He shoved the cash deep into his pocket, unrolled the notes remaining in his fist and as they fanned like a mating peacock, he not so much offered but condescended: 'Let me buy you a drink for your well-meaning effort, though.'

The evening, predictably, got blurry thereafter. Armadillo wasn't a bad drunk: he rarely caused offence and despite the bravado of young men inviting him, provoking him, to fight, always maintained enough self-control to avoid flattening one of the pretenders. How then was it the next thing he became aware of was waking up to the midday sun, forcing harsh rays in splinters through the shutters of an unfamiliar hotel room?

*

Despite the whirr of the overhead fan, it was a challenge to breathe. He was convinced the air supply to the room was restricted. The air in his lungs lingering at the bottom, in the shallows, forcing halitosis into his mouth. He lay on his back awhile watching the blades of the fan spin relentlessly, wondering. Like a detective, he felt ready to search for clues. He also felt like a victim, but he was unsure why.

Sweat sat in stagnant puddles in the crevices of his semi-naked body. He felt disgusted, maybe with himself or maybe someone else. Threads of thoughts were just beyond his reach as he told himself to count to ten and then commence working out precisely where he was. When he reached the count of ten, he gave himself the breathing space of another ten. Then standing quickly, far too quickly for his head and body to work in harmony, the room tipped first one way, then the other, then back again, never levelling between the sway. Was the unrelenting motion of this curious room caused by it being aboard some floating vessel?

Somehow, he made it to the window; holding tight to the cracked wooden frame he drew back the velour curtains, noticing how the sun had faded the fabric like the stripes on the haunches of an ageing tiger. The panorama presented to him, blurred with a haziness partly due to the sun beginning to kiss the horizon, combined with the long-accumulated sheen of grime on the outside of the window. Running his index finger across the glass he found to his disgust that the dirt was also on the inside. He wiped the smudge with the hem of his t-shirt, instinctively he somehow didn't want to leave any trace of himself, any evidence, as if this were a crime scene waiting to be investigated.

Taking stock of the view beyond the grime: a city, maybe a town. A handful of tall buildings in rows, mostly low rise, two-storey. A scattering of neglected trees. A dual carriageway, merging into single lanes. A few cars honking with languorous impatience. A church with its doors tightly shut. Several pedestrians, mostly solo men walking with purpose. One family with two small children clutching their parents' hands. A hill rising behind the buildings, peppered with dwellings. No landmarks. Nothing of any exception. He could be in any town. Any place.

He needed coffee to override the strange, bitter taste in his mouth. And some pills to stop the pressure building inside his head. Turning back into the room, it looked even more sordid than when he had awoken. His clothes were strewn across the moss-green carpet which he instinctively knew had looked cheap from the first day it had been laid. He couldn't bring himself to inspect the disarray on the bed; something about it knotted his stomach. Shame was unfamiliar: on the rare occasions he had experienced it, he had little accumulated resilience to drive it away. His mind conjured his wife, neatly dressed as always with earrings matching her necklace. He pushed this wholesome image away: she did not belong here.

Locating the green plastic hotel phone firmly fixed to the wall, he dialled zero, the universal route to connect to reception. After three shrill rings, an impatient voice answered, 'Yes?'

'Hello. Could I order a pot of strong black coffee? No milk but some sugar please.'

'We don't have room service. There's a café on the corner: turn right outside. But they don't reopen until five.'

Wondering exactly what it was he had thanked the disembodied voice for, he replaced the receiver. Sitting on the edge of the bed, the sensation of his feet being more firmly on the floor now, he surveyed the room once more with a greater scrutiny. The minibar door was swinging on its hinges, leaving a defrosted puddle adding yet one more stain to the carpet. Its contents were scattered amok in a scene of sordid hedonism—two drained vodka bottles lay flirtatiously close to a half-empty foil packet of salted peanuts. Other bottles were strewn greedily across the table, their caps looking jaunty as children's playthings. Amongst this debris sat glasses. Two tumblers, side by side. One had filmy fingerprints on the chunky glass, the other displayed an accusatory lipsticked imprint on the rim.

Armadillo sat back on the edge of the bed, forcing his mind to at least piece a chain of events, a faded conversation, any clue that led him to this hole. His mind gently served him measured doses just small enough for him to swallow without choking.

It felt impossible for him to distinguish whether his feelings of sordidness were due to this current predicament or flashbacks to the other three times during his marriage he had indulged his lust in cheap hotel rooms. Relocating to the bathroom he threw water over his face after running it to a temperature cold enough to inflict punishment. The coarse, threadbare towels had been strewn across the lino, and as he patted his face dry the sense of contamination from them merely added to his shame. Facing his reflection in the mirror, he addressed himself: *What have you done? What brought you to this hole? Who brought you to this hole?*

On meeting his stare he couldn't fail to notice how, sitting within the tapestry of blotches and stubble, were two widely dilated pupils staring back like puddles under streetlights on a winter's evening. He dropped his gaze, aware he was humiliating himself. And then he saw the cliché of a ruby red lipstick kiss imprinted at the bottom righthand corner of the mirror. A flashback. A woman's sultry lips hypnotising him as they formed around a straw impaled in a long, orange drink. The memory slipped out of his reach once more, leaving a dark shadow.

He had to get out. He had to get back to his troupe and distract his mind with hard physical training—he had to sweat out this toxicity.

Picking up his deflated trousers, he pulled them on, finding his shirt tangled within the bedsheets. One sock was easy to find but the second had gone astray. The least of his worries. He pulled off the first in a fit of irritation and pushed his naked feet into his shoes. With reclaimed control he searched the room one last time for any lingering possessions that might incriminate him. He shook out the sheets: nothing. Banging open drawers of the bedside table, the only item he found was a Holy Bible, sat judgmentally in the corner of the top one. He fell to his knees to search beneath the bed. The long-settled dust came as no surprise. He needed air.

Turning towards the door he patted his trouser pockets once, twice, three times. Empty. A flash of lightning struck his brain as he recalled propping up a bar, seeing a vision of himself showing off the rolls of his prize money as a rooster plumps its feathers. It had bulged in his pockets and hands. Even when graciously buying a round for the bar, he still couldn't have spent it all. *Think, think. Cast your mind back, see what fragments you can catch. Where the hell is the money?* He recalled phoning Julia at the end of the match, making promises that he could now as a suddenly wealthy man, take the whole family on a beach holiday, rent a villa with an ocean view, eat crayfish for lunch and lobster for dinner. A gesture of compensation for the weeks of his absence. The children squealing in the background. A warm sensation flooding his veins. He had become the husband, the father, the man his own father never was.

In the corridor, the lift lingered too long in its creaky ascent. Impatience got the better of him, so he took the stairs, three at a time until he arrived at a reception with ideas above its station. Dark wooden panels had been polished like a church lectern while the grey marble floor created the impression of tasteful luxury. He despised its deceitfulness. Standing behind the high desk awash with tourist leaflets lurked a youngish man, who Armadillo felt sure smirked on seeing him.

'Ah sir,' he said obsequiously, 'are you checking out of room 31?' The lady said you would be settling the bill.'

He knew this man was party to key bits of information about 'the lady' and was treading a fragile path between discretion and mockery, yet Armadillo's few remaining fragments of pride prevented him from asking for more information.

'Of course,' he said, playing his allotted role in this charade. 'The thing is, I don't have my wallet and I'm afraid she must have forgotten this. Can I return later and settle up?'

'I'm afraid we don't permit that within our checking out policy,' clipped the young man with authority beyond his age. 'You could do so if you leave an item for security. A ring? A watch maybe?'

Armadillo knew even before he reached for his right wrist that he would feel an indent in his flesh where his late father's watch used to reassuringly sit .

'Very well,' he conceded, as he slipped off his worn, golden wedding band.

*

Josefina made as much noise as possible for a woman entering the small hallway of an apartment. She tugged her keys out of the lock, clanking metal against metal, kicking the door shut with her left foot, the momentum causing it to rattle against the cheap metal frame. She dropped her bag on the floor while simultaneously throwing her keys into a glass bowl atop the cheap pine bench.

'Sebastian, are you up?' she shrilled.

'How did it go?' he replied, his voice projected above the cacophony of a TV soap opera playing in a room at the far end of the hallway.

'Fine. I need a shower. Whatever you do, don't get up off your arse.'

The bathroom door slammed shut behind her.

By the time Sebastian had hauled himself upright and meandered over to permit the doorframe of the room to support his bodyweight, all he could hear was water spurting out of the shower head in angry bursts. He knew she would have the water temperature punishingly high. He shrugged.

Turning to resume his horizontal sofa position, he gazed down at his own body as if witnessing it through the eyes of another. It was crumpled, rumpled. Lifting the hem of his t-shirt to his nose, he verified his suspicion of a dank odour emitting from his pores. The eyes which met him in the sharp, cheap glass of the mirror disapproved as his hand ran through a knotted thatch of uncombed hair and down to the coarseness of four-day old chin stubble. And yet, he still congratulated this reflection on looking rugged and rather manly. He turned to admire his profile.

'You've still got it dude,' he reassured his mirror image. Turning back to wink mischievously at himself, he conceded: 'Maybe a wash wouldn't go amiss though.' His voice was almost as grating as the way he rattled the bathroom door, calling out: 'Are you going to be long in there? I was about to have a shower when you came in. I have to get to work later.'

No reply. He shrugged and turned back towards the direction of the lounge, the sofa, the TV, the undrawn curtains keeping daylight at bay, but hesitated as he spotted Josefina's handbag flopping on the floor like a small dog sleeping in the shade of a summer's day. Picking it up, he sank his exploratory fingers into its interior like a surgeon checking a patient's vital organs. His fingers touched and squeezed various items in turn: a worn leather purse, the sharp bristles of a hairbrush stabbing under his fingernails, the unmistakable shape of a lipstick, a random key, another lipstick. Why do women carry around so much crap? And then his fingers made contact with the purpose of his pursuit, first with a brief touch and then with a caress. A roll of banknotes secured with an elastic band. Hang on… there was another. Two juicy rolls of crisp new notes. He grabbed them in the greedy way an infant seizes a parents' fingers. The hallway was too dimly lit for him to check them out; instead he satisfied himself by examining their weight. They reminded him of big cigars.

Another bang on the bathroom door. 'Hurry up babe—we're going out for breakfast.'

*

The spitting spray from the lime-scaled shower head couldn't be hot enough to provide Josefina with the punishment she craved. Resting her forehead on the cold tiles, she watched her guilt drain down the plughole. But still she didn't feel clean. She turned off the water and wrapped herself in her old brittle towel. She drew deep breaths into the deeper part of her lungs as she sat on the closed toilet seat lid and slowly muttered, 'Leave me alone. Please, please leave me alone.'

Looking at the crumpled clothes on the floor, the black stockings lying in two lonely puddles, the pushup lacy bra and dress that somehow managed to still look tight fitting even when absent of a body. She felt overwhelmed: it was a costume, a workplace uniform from which she had to detach herself. Although merely inanimate objects, they somehow spoke judgmental words to her. They were silenced by her harsh kick jettisoning the pile into a corner behind the toilet. Looking at the rumpled heap, her mind cast back to the image of hastily discarded shorts and t-shirts—debris on a beach when as a child her father left work early to surprise her by collecting her from school, driving to where the sea kissed the edge of the earth, and they could watch the waves. Squealing and kicking waves with delight until her lips turned blue, her father would bribe her out of the sea with the promise of hot chocolate on their way home. A secret between them, kept conspiratorially from her mother.

Without fail she would fall asleep in the passenger seat of the car as her father drove home, avoiding as many bumps in the road as possible. She would forever remember the sensation of safety when, on arrival, he would gather her in his large arms, a precious bundle, shushing her murmurs as he slid her body between cool, cotton sheets where she would relish delicious sandy feet and salty hair.

'Babe, have you fallen asleep in there?' The question jolted her out of her reverie.

Josefina released the lock and peered out at him. 'Can I just have five minutes in peace? Just five minutes on my own. Please.'

'Okay. Okay. There's no need to be so tetchy. Relax a bit babe. You've done your job, you've got the dough, you can relax for a bit now.'

Closing the door on him she rested her spine against the comforting solidity of the wood. Deep breaths. A few more and then she could face the world again. She was far from being able to face her own reflection in the mirror. 'Needs must,' she muttered to herself. 'Needs must.'

*

Whenever they treated themselves to breakfast Sebastian liked to choose the cafe. He would wander the pavement past each, checking which waiters were on duty. Once he was assured there was at least one who would recognise him from his previous life as a member of their tribe, he would steer Josefina by the elbow to a prominent pavement seat, where they could both see and be seen. Whatever the intensity of sunshine on the given day, he would always sport his sunglasses along with a neatly ironed shirt, the collar slightly turned up, designer jeans, loafers, no socks.

Even though the waiters had seen and acknowledged his presence, he would still shout them over with a raised hand, stopping just short of clicking his fingers.

The waiters in turn played their role: solicitous, courteous, but stopping short of obsequiousness. The charade placed them into an ambivalent position: they knew they were being patronised, but also to play along would undoubtedly be rewarded with a sizeable tip. Sebastian was renowned for tips which conveyed his intention: I have money to spare. See how I was once one of you and now I am on a higher level.

It was a small town in which families knew and oftentimes interfered in each other's business. It was known that he used to wait tables, serve behind late night bars, sometimes pulling a double shift to pay his way through his chemistry degree. *So*, folks wondered, sometimes alone, but frequently in small gaggles, *where was this surplus income coming from?* Had he landed a job with one of the big pharma companies, this being one of the few industries still thriving? As the recession bit, good people had increasingly dark thoughts. Minds went to places of little hope, where imagined harms dwelt— sometimes inflicted on others but more often on the self. Big pharma companies could then step in with small, easy to swallow tablets offering respite and hope.

One other idea locals shared to explain Sebastian's newly found habit of generous tipping—the woman he was now always seen with was wealthy. It was noted that she was a little older than him, and when together there was a degree of awkwardness between them that suggested their relationship was built more on an exchange of mutual benefit than mutual passion. Maybe he was a paid escort? Although he didn't appear sufficiently solicitous, and she didn't seem sufficiently joyful.

As the public spectacle of these breakfasts continued, they noted a nebulous resentment typical of codependent relationships built on an equal tension between love and hate. Not one observer had a fanciful enough imagination to guess the truth—after all, life is so much stranger than fiction.

Eight

The on-the-edge reckless delight typical of the wrestlers' tours had been replaced by disappointment, a currency of deflation mixed with anxiety and topped with anticipatory grief. Everything was falling apart.

When the bright fibres of joy, adoration and success holding the wrestling tour together unravelled, there was a certain inevitability in the need to sit back and surrender. It needed to take its course; to resist it would merely divert the river's path down a different hillside, but it would eventually meander to meet the same ocean. One way or another.

Emiliano struggled to swim with this tide. Everything he had built was crumbling. Born into a life in which Maria eked out the available food into meagre portions, his growing feet crushed in tight shoes and never having the bus fare to get to school, his fear of one day returning to this poverty was deeply embedded in his psyche.

'Control what you can control and let go of that which you can't,' Maria often repeated to him, one of her many mottos to soften the brutality of life. But right now he felt as if very little was within his control. And this made him tetchy. After a few attempts to buoy him up, his fellow wrestlers made an unspoken pact to leave him to stew in his own juices.

He wasn't alone in his tetchiness—most of the troupe were out of sorts. When one of their own sustained an injury, vulnerability pervaded all, no matter the attempts at suppression with machismo and false confidence. Lillibet had mended: at least the collagen and calcium in her femur had knotted itself together. The healing of her spirit was a different matter, however: she snapped at the slightest perceived sleight, dealt harshly with inanimate objects (cutlery, the kettle, doors, lamps), enough clatter to wake the sleeping gods. Despite Consuelo's need to end protestations, her daughter still overtrained, punishing this body which had, for the first time in her life, let her down.

Pilar didn't have the luxury of physical and emotional space to prevent herself becoming sucked into Lillibet's dissonance. The best she could do was erect an emotional barricade. She was, however, hardly trouble-free herself. The pervading anxiety about the pending economic crash filtered through to her each day now. If ticket sales continued to plummet, what would happen to the rest of the tour? Where would her income come from if Lillibet didn't get back into the ring soon? And as for Gabriel! Having been seduced by the romantic notion he was her soulmate, her best friend, her lover, her thoughts had led her to imagine the children they would conceive: two girls and a boy. The girls would have his height, balanced with her voluptuous hips and thick, lustrous hair—an outward display of her fertility which would lead this daughter to bear her own offspring. Pilar's grandchildren. She found the boy harder to manifest in physical form, so she focused on the sharpness of his brain and tenderness of his nature. So vividly had she imagined these small beings her grief at the loss of Gabriel was compounded by the accompanying loss of these imaginary babies.

The only member of the troupe unaffected by the changes in their fortunes was Emilio. Little provoked his emotions, not due to a Zen-like state of serenity but his long-term habit of suppressing feelings. His emotions sat buried like a forgotten tuber: unless someone tenacious and courageous dug deep into the compacted soil, they were unlikely to be exposed to the sunlight again. Like the showman he was, he faced the world with lips stretched widely in the imitation of a smile.

In short, there were fractures in the fabric that had woven the luchadores so tightly together. Fractures where bad energy seeped in, initially unnoticed until it had spread like a cancer. Before anyone paid attention the corrosive damage had been done.

*

The fissures eventually penetrated even Emilio's calm. Repeated attempts to visit Lillibet's hospital bed only to be ejected by the now overly solicitous matron were undeniable. Something had broken. Something beautiful had turned rotten. He couldn't let the others witness this heartbreak: they would tease him, treat him like a child. Especially Emiliano. Emilio would not, under any circumstances, be the object of his taunting again. He reflected how in the embryonic days of their wrestling career, Maria would apply a comfrey compress with a mother's love onto his stumped thumb after each match, that weakness exploited by his opponents. Pressed, punched, and trodden upon.

He sensed how much Maria loved these solitary times with her quiet boy. The bathing and tending allowed her to cling onto foregone maternal days, when her twins were babes and she was their sun and moon. Emilio, in turn, let down his guard and reverted to being her boy child for a couple of hours. He allowed her this indulgence; it sated his need to feel safe, to be held.

Two train rides and a bus took him back to the village of his childhood. His arrival mid-afternoon gave him the solitude he craved. All the nosey neighbours were taking their siestas behind closed shutters, leaving him free to arrive with his only observers, a couple of lazy dogs, tails flicking flies from their haunches in the dusty shade of shop doorways.

*

Age was not so much sneaking up on Maria as arriving like an uninvited guest in the dead of night. The pressure she had put on her younger body took its toll; the weight of her twins during their nine months' occupancy of her womb, their pushing, squeezing, panting births, had contorted her belly and uterus into shapes familiar only to womankind. This had been followed and compounded by the physicality of housework, washing clothes by hand, sweeping, polishing, lifting her infant boys, carrying food and firewood from the market three times a week, mothering: the plight of most women across the globe. Her sacrifice of the most nutritious food her tight budget allowed to her boys left her body depleted of vitamins and minerals. In short, she was tired. Body and soul.

She creaked in unfamiliar places when shifting from

sitting. Ascending the hill the contours of which stretched from the village square to her house, she now had to stop several times to catch her breath, out of pride, disguising this as lingering to admire the view behind her.

Her skin was drying, her elbows resembled used sandpaper, the crevices between her fingers needed continual massaging with oils and unguents, and her cheeks became chapped at the slightest easterly wind. And gravity exerted an ever-stronger pull on her breasts and jowls. The word 'jowls' had never been part of her inner vocabulary until a couple of years ago, but now she whispered it sadly to herself every time she looked in the mirror.

Since Juan Carlos' departure, Maria didn't have a life companion to remind her tenderly that beneath those bodily deteriorations she was still a beautiful woman who had borne children into this world and had her wisdom etched on her face for all to honour. Instead, all she could hear was her own self-critical voice, speaking in increasingly screeching tones, answering her back when not requested: so full of sharp opinions, of criticisms.

During her solitary evenings, Maria knitted garments—sweaters, scarves, gloves, all for her boys, knowing they would never wear them. Partly because she was producing so many, knitting an endless skein of multi-coloured yarns into repeated shapes, and partly because deep down she knew that in their new lives the twins were embarrassed by these homespun garments. These days they wore city clothes, mass-produced, imported from lands neither she nor they would step foot in, stitched in unventilated factories by mothers wearing down their fingertips and souls just to feed the child who slept on a rug on the dusty floor at her feet. But her boys preferred the cocoon of this anonymity in which the transaction of money for goods meant an absence of emotional debt, an absence of maternal love stitched into the seams.

But still Maria continued winding and unwinding her skeins of wool—for where else could the love she contained in her heart go?

When the twins phoned her, she feigned understanding about their busy lives, preventing them from visiting. She carefully followed the news of their wrestling victories in newspapers and on the radio, sharing it with neighbours pretending she had garnered the word first-hand from her sons. The announcement of each victorious match brought a swell to her chest, even if it caught in her throat like a fish bone, a double-edged sword, for it was these successes which transported her babes to lands foreign to her, beyond her reach.

Cheques arrived in the post, dropping lightly on her doorstep, unpredictably yet frequently. No one could accuse her boys of being mean. Maria carefully folded each cheque neatly in half and placed them in a small-battered metal tin, previously a gaudily painted vessel for fancy biscuits. She secured the hinged lid and placed it in a seldom-used drawer in the unlit corner of the kitchen. Neither Emilio or Emiliano raised the issue of the uncashed cheques during their phone calls, and she wondered if they had noticed that these generous sums were never deducted from their bank accounts. Maria's familiarity with frugality lived uninterrupted as a pattern within her bones and muscles. While not always perfect, the familiar nevertheless provided her with endless comfort.

Emilio's unexpected arrival threw her off balance. She faltered on seeing her quiet boy standing on her doorstep—why was he here? What had initiated this unexpected visit? Her instinct was not to question further but to open her arms. It was into these open arms that Emilio fell as heavy sobs wracked his body.

'It's okay,' she soothed, stroking his hair. 'Whatever it is, we can mend it together.'

'I love her mum, with all my heart. And I believe she loves me, but she won't let me near. She has hardened her kind heart against me and I don't know why.'

'Come inside,' she said as she led him gently into his childhood kitchen. 'Sit.'

She pulled out a chair tucked neatly under the table. 'Cry as much as you like, then you can tell me all about her.'

Emilio surrendered to the warmth of maternal love.

*

Over a tender week's impasse from the outside world, Maria filled her son with enough love that he was once more outwardly a functioning human being. The return train journey had been a time for reflection: the repetitive metal on metal as the wheels turned on the rails had soothed him. The train carriages were half empty—folks were not travelling so much—tight budgets meant fewer family holidays, and those who had money would never be seen travelling on the public rail system.

He had managed to secure a window seat in a carriage with just one other man seated opposite, slyly studying his companion's appearance. Sadly, Emilio was accustomed to being observed as if he were an embodied walking freak show. But becoming used to something over the course of a lifetime doesn't make it easier to bear. On the contrary, being subjected to constant staring and unspoken yet evident judgements became wearing. Very wearing.

Sitting back as far in his seat as possible, he feigned nonchalance. The top of his head fell short of the antimacassar protecting the seat, while his feet swung way above the floor.

'Can I help you?' he asked the staring man, his tone polite but firm.

The man seemed surprised to be addressed. Looking around as if the words had been spoken by another passenger, he flushed above his worn shirt collar like a misbehaving child. This momentary disruption of both the air and the atmosphere created an opportunity for Emilio to study the man, assessing both the physical and intellectual challenge he could be facing. He noted:

-forest green well-worn trousers.

-leather boots carelessly laced.

-a jacket with sleeves too long, probably donated by another man of larger build, even possibly stolen.

-a pork pie hat held in his lap.

-a bushy moustache, stubbly chin, stray hairs poking aggressively from his nose and ears.

-small, piggy eyes.

-an old watch, leather-strapped, fraying at the edges.

-no rings, not even a wedding band.

Emilio's wrestling had taught him the skill of quickly sizing up an opponent, sussing points of weakness, cataloguing vulnerabilities. He could easily take this man down: he could floor him bodily, outwit him verbally. He also knew this man had made the same assumption about himself, based solely on his size. By nature Emilio wasn't adversarial, but he was at the end of life's tether, and staring from the end of this tether was a rude, obnoxious man.

'I said, can I help you?' he repeated with a staccato rhythm.

The man shifted his weight from buttock to buttock looking down at his feet. Staring straight into his face, Emilio defied him to look up. *What do you think you're seeing? May the discomfiture be yours not mine from now on.*

The claustrophobic air was lifted by the guard sliding open the carriage door.

'Tickets please,' he requested leaning his tall frame against the weighted door—lackadaisical, bored, pride in his job having evaporated years hence. There was a brief piece of theatre in which tickets were sought from pockets, duly inspected, stamped and returned, the guard moving along the corridor to repeat the exercise in the adjacent carriage, and the next, and next, a dissipating echo down the corridor.

Both passengers were grateful for the intrusion: as the tension between them subsided, they were able to resume the business typical of rail passengers, studiously ignoring each other. Had Emilio enjoyed the luxury of dotage, he might, on a quiet evening, when the day's sun was fading, have reflected on this as a pivotal life's moment. A moment to tell the grandchildren he would never have.

'That was the moment everything changed—when everything inside of me became clearer and shifted.' For it was at that moment Emilio realised he no longer cared what people thought of him. All those years of wondering, worrying, melted like a blancmange on a summer's afternoon. Nothing mattered. He had lost Lillibet, so what else could matter now? He stopped asking himself what he had done wrong, what, in another time and place, he could have done differently. He accepted fate. He still knew Lillibet was beautiful, despite or maybe because of her flaws. He still loved her complex heart with its muddle of vulnerability and forcefulness. But if he could no longer secure her approval, never mind love, what did the opinions of others matter in this life?

The abrupt relinquishment of those years of caring since he was a child, years of critical self-judgement, was liberating. His raw emotions, however, surged in an acute, hot bundle. Without a critical voice swirling in his head, he was better able to hear the external world: the cluck clunk of the train's metal wheels against track, the scratch of branches against the window, the wheeze of the man's shallow breathing. The volume of the world had been amplified. Scents also pervaded his nostrils—some mouldy fruit was in the vicinity, but the aroma emitting from his own pores was surprisingly sweet. His body felt lighter. So this was liberation? This was the state in which most people made their way through the world. Was this how his brother always experienced life—the twin who had always felt little need for external validation. How could he make use of these new sensations, this freedom from self-criticism?

Emilio had forever carried these fraternal dynamics like someone dons a well-worn overcoat through each changing season—it wasn't smart or attractive, but provided comfort in its familiarity. Itchy and mostly uncomfortable, yet functional. And he felt cold and exposed without it, because it had provided him some protection from the outside world by allowing him not to have to grow his own shell. Emilio had never learned the skills of valuing something until it was gone, and now in its absence he felt liberated and exposed.

As the train drew into Emilio's destination, he sensed the man's eyes through the train window, watching him with a penetrating gaze as he disembarked. The gap between the train and platform was too large for the range of Emilio's stride. His leather case thudded as he threw it onto the platform, then in an uncharacteristic act of public showmanship beyond the wrestling ring, he sprang into a full somersault. Landing neatly on two feet, he turned and waved to his startled observer. Without a backward glance he picked up his case and sauntered the platform towards the exit, knowing his fun was over, and it was time to face up to… what exactly? He wasn't sure what dynamic would be in play once he returned to the troupe, but he sensed enough to evoke a feeling of deep unsettledness in the pit of his stomach.

*

As soon as Emilio returned from his visit to their mother, Emiliano sensed a large shift within his brother. He had somehow grown taller, even though when they stood side by side their eyes remained on the same level. If not height, what? His brother somehow took up more space in the world. And unapologetically. He was breathing in more oxygen: did this therefore leave less for himself in his zero sum of their dynamic?

Inevitably, Emiliano wondered what had taken place during this visit—what had passed between Emilio and their mother that made his twin bolder? To enquire would cause him to make the admission that of late he had been neglecting his mother, restricting his contact; and secondly it would make real the fissure between the twins, it would name it and force them to acknowledge that over the passage of time it had become wider and less traversable.

Best not to voice this, to speak it into reality. Best to keep quiet. For now.

Nine

'Are you sure you've got the formula correct?' asked Josefina, leaning on the kitchen doorframe, her arms folded just below her breasts which were barely covered in a purple silk kimono.

'Of course I have,' Sebastian replied, his tone gentler than his words. 'You do your job, I'll do mine. Speaking of which…' He cast his eyes up and down her body letting her know he'd taken in her dishevelled state of semi-undress: unwashed, limp hair, smeared mascara, her shins showing a visible shadow of patchy stubble. 'You don't exactly look ready to do your job.'

Studiously she ignored this comment, unwilling to concede that power to him. With power came control, wrapped up in a neat package. She must protect her ground in this relationship. Just because she needed to don her seductress's outfit didn't give him permission to play the role of the pimp.

'I think it was too strong last time.'

'How do you know that? Are you a chemist now?'

With a small silver teaspoon historically used to administer absinthe, he dropped white, finely ground powder into the clear liquid. One spoon, two spoons and one more for luck. They had to make sure their victim was merely knocked out for a few hours—just long enough for their life to be destroyed by scandal, span out in salacious newspaper reports. Just long enough for their wife to be appalled and possibly file for divorce by the end of the year.

Josefina had adopted the habit of prohibiting newspapers from her apartment. She remembered reading crime stories in which the offender had pulled off the perfect heist, the perfect murder, the perfect forgery, only to be arrested when the police, armed with a search warrant and an overdeveloped superiority, discover a stack of newspapers, headlines of the crimes circled with an incriminating pen. Rather she had taken to lingering at kiosks, choosing a different one each time, to check the reporter's glee-infused headlines, full of an intoxicating mix for the perfect story to increase the paper's circulation: an athletic wrestler's whore, a seedy hotel room, a drugging, a robbery. Even the sloppiest of reporters could paint a picture worthy of a film reel projecting onto the irises and imaginations of every greedy reader.

Careful not to enter the speculative gossip of the gathering crowd around the kiosk, she heard the rise and fall of chatter and felt vicarious excitement. A sour taste of nausea rose in Josefina's oesophagus.

She refocused her mind on Sebastian and his concoction mixing.

'But the last guy was out for too long. You said he would only be unconscious a couple of hours—I watched him for three hours before it was too risky to hang around longer. There was absolutely no sign of him stirring when I left.'

'Okay so we know he didn't leave the hotel for another

five hours after you left—I checked with the receptionist. It doesn't mean he was out cold all that time.' Irritation mixed with anxiety crept into Sebastian's voice: if Josefina lost her nerve, their ploy would be in jeopardy, never mind his future as a research scientist and life as a free man. Sadly his emotional range was too limited to realise that what was presenting in his accomplice as anxiety was actually the manifestation of a tortured conscience. His mind was distracted by the prize money and the egotistical confirmation he was able to calculate the exact dosage of barbiturates to knock out a fully grown man for a short period.

He had never stopped to consider the picture of the Madonna smiling beatifically from the kitchen wall just above the shelf housing Josefina's mugs was more than decoration. He had never spent a long wakeful night with this woman, listening to her, gently encouraging her to articulate her values, dreams, principles. He had no appreciation of the catholic conscience that ran deep through her soul like an eternal fire. In building a relationship founded purely on a codependent need to financially survive, Josefina and Sebastian failed to plant the roots from which mutual understanding grew.

'I'm just saying...' she just said.

'Hush with your worries—I've got this.'

'But what if one night you get the dosage wrong? We only want to rob them, don't we? We don't mean them actual harm.'

'Hush, I said.' He silenced her with a perfunctory kiss, which she tolerated, just. As his lips pressed hot and dry against hers, she thought of how in novels, films, fictional worlds, criminal enterprise between lovers was fuelled by a certain eroticism. The sharing of mutual danger linked the couple with frenzied libidos. With her, the opposite was true: where she had once felt a degree of attraction to Sebastian's body, his muscular torso, his long, slender fingers, that gym-tightened butt she had first admired in his waiter's trousers, she now felt a degree of repulsion bordering on contempt. In her mind she cut off the thought that she could be projecting disappointment in herself: this was not the life and career she had imagined in her London days, and neither had she thought that her talent for seduction would one day be a means to retain a roof over her head rather than a form of pleasure and fun.

She pushed a hand into his chest to signify the end of the kiss.

'I must get ready. The wrestlers will all be in the bar soon. The window of opportunity between them being a bit tipsy and downright drunk is a narrow one.'

'Sure. Okay. The magic concoction is almost ready.'

They were back on the territory of co-conspirators rather than lovers. Better to keep it that way, she thought, better all round.

*

Their evening was the same but different. The twins had easily won their bout. Emilio's newfound confidence translated into a forceful energy in the ring. Emiliano was compelled to match his brother's enthusiasm to the delight of the crowd and the joy of those who had placed bets on this win. The twins ducked and danced, tumbled, and slammed their tight, compact bodies into their opponents.

Their tags had been spot on: perfect timing, rapid enough to catch the others off guard, one red mask rolling beneath the ropes at the precise moment that one blue mask vaulted over them in perfect choreography. The match, short-lived, had reached a predictable conclusion: the twins were on fire.

Meanwhile, busy preparing for her return to the ring that same evening, Lillibet was conscious her injury had left an uncomfortable echo in her muscles and soft tissues. No longer able to fully trust her body, an unfamiliar vulnerability haunted her.

On the previous day Miguel, a perceptive man attuned to his protégé, attempted a discussion with her, to reassure her that these feelings would pass. But Lillibet shut him down, feigning a concern over choosing her outfit: the yellow taffeta petticoat might be more suitable, combined with the emerald skirt, or maybe the oxblood red skirt would be better, although that could clash too much with the yellow... To allow Miguel to open an honest conversation would involve her relaxing the walls of defence she had so carefully erected, brick by brick, in the many days spent in her hospital bed.

Her pre-match preparations were steady and systematic. Pilar silently watched as her friend moved around the caravan with a precision typical of the superstitious, touching objects several times. She placed a jade stone, gifted to her years ago by Consuelo, deep inside her skirt pocket where she could touch its reassuring smooth coldness. These new rituals consumed the time and filled Pilar with anxious thoughts Lillibet would not be able to make her way over to the main arena in time. Reluctant to create more pressure than already filled the air like the static buildup prior to an electrical storm, she closely watched the long hand of the wall clock as it dragged out the minutes, uttering a quiet prayer that she would not have to intervene in these new ritualistic preparations.

Lillibet was desperate to avoid crossing paths with the twins, which could incite a conversation with one, or worse, both. There might be accusations about what passed between them. Or what could have developed. There was a gulf between what had once been, what might have been, and what was. Worse, she was unclear how to untangle ambivalent feelings of attraction and shame. She no longer understood herself. Life and its complexities invaded her carefully constructed straightforward worldview and penetrated her marrow like bindweed. It was best to keep her mind focused on the task, namely getting her body back in the ring to fight like a warrior woman. Lillibet stroked the jade stone.

Pilar and Lillibet both noticed the roar that arose from the arena. Up, up, into the humid night, like unscrewing the lid of a violently shaken bottle of lemonade. The release was palpable: box office numbers were low this evening as people held tight to spare cash for fear that their wallets, once emptied, might never be refilled. There were fewer people in the crowd, but a loud, raucous cry told them something out of the ordinary was arousing them.

*

Emiliano experienced a swell of unexpected pride as he watched his brother, both arms raised as if to draw the spotlight on himself and accept the adoration from the crowd. He had played his part in arousing the audience, jumping the ropes into the ring when tagged by his brother, knocking his opponent to the deck with swerving, grasping hands and then skipping to their corner to tag in return. Yet his twin was the star with his display of unrelenting grace and propulsive energy, until the referee counted descending numbers to the accompanying chorus from the crowd. The slap of the ref's palm flat on the sprung deck signalled the defeat of the rudos and the victory of the technicos, but the acclaim belonged to Emilio who had metaphorically and literally stepped into the spotlight. His twin, always the crowd-pleaser, ducked below the ropes to enter the ring as the referee sank to one knee to level their height differential, joining the line of glory, flanked by the small yet powerful wrestlers, arms linked and raised.

This brotherly pride was disorientating. Emiliano took care not to meet his brother's eyes for fear of amplifying this vulnerability; instead his wide grin was directed outwards towards their adoring public. The Conquestas' prize money had been earned. This prize so much more than the crisp notes: it was pride and glory. If only he could open his heart wide enough to allow this swell of emotion.

*

To control the confusion before it controlled him, Emiliano decided not to analyse the change in Emilio's behaviour. He had lived life on the surface, superficially, never learning the skills needed to dive beneath any torrent of swirling emotion. Rather he chose to play the fool, the drunkard. So now he was devoid of the necessary ability to read the nuance between his brother's presenting behaviour and inner state. It wasn't his fault though he felt life hadn't been easy. *All things considered,* he reassured himself, *you have done well to be as good a son as possible, to be a success in the highly competitive wrestling field, and to have friends and compatriots. You are undoubtedly a victor.*

Emiliano wasn't the only one filled with regret at the loss of Lillibet's attentions—Emilio was also carrying a heavy heart comprised of broken fragments. The only difference was that his fragments had sharp, jagged edges designed to keep future love and pain at bay, whereas his brother's fractured heart was still soft and accepting.

When the twins had changed, rubbed down their sweaty bodies with cold, damp flannels, and completed their transformation from performers to everyday men, Emiliano merely nodded as his brother was the one to herald the cry of, 'Let's get out and explore the bars in this town before they pull down the shutters!'

Ironically, Emiliano for once, wasn't in the mood for people, noise, interaction. Instead, more typically, he needed a strong drink or three. He was still riding this curious wave of strange protectiveness towards his brother, even though Emilio appeared not to need it. So caught in his own tumult, he lacked the capacity to stand back and acknowledge the mutual rebound from Lillibet's rejection they were both experiencing. It was a curious bond. The scar tissue was still too delicately knitted to risk splitting the wound again, yet, like a child who picks at a scab on his knee caused by a fall from a malevolent bicycle, he still wondered and hoped Lillibet might be present in the bar that evening. The only sighting he had made of her today was to spy her from behind the velvet curtain as she gloriously swung her opponent above her head in a swirl of peacock skirts and petticoats.

Maybe, if they were to accidentally bump into each other in a social setting, she would soften, perhaps providing some explanation for the withdrawal of her attention. Maybe, just maybe.

*

Seconds before Emilio arrived at the bar, the rain came down, creating a sheen on the expansive windowpanes through which he spied too much gaudy neon. He never understood why these bars felt the compulsion to announce everything with bright lights. This was not the time for critical thinking, however, but for the new, bold Emilio to step up. The Emilio of action.

'One beer, a tall one please.' On entering the bar, he projected his voice to reach the solo barman. 'And whatever the others want—no doubles though!' The barman was the sort whose stomach arrived in the room before him. He dried his hands on a grubby tea towel draped over his left shoulder and set about delivering this order.

Emilio swept his arm generously in the direction of his compatriot wrestlers while patting his inside pocket in assurance that his chunky roll of banknote winnings was safely tucked inside like a much-loved baby in her cot.

The luchadores, having enthusiastically arrived at the bar a full twenty minutes ahead of the twins, raised a swathe of eyebrows to each other in a hirsute ripple. One even looked overtly down at Emilio's right hand to check if he had a missing digit, or if the man before him was the fully digited brother. Not prone to looking a gift horse in the mouth, the wrestlers in turn shrugged and shouted their orders at a rate too rapid for the poor bartender to keep pace. For too many orders were for doubles.

Emilio, making full use of his highly toned upper body strength, swung himself atop a stool beside the jukebox, and, in emptying his pocket of coins, lined up a medley of fast tempo beats.

Josefina was already sitting tall on another stool in that very bar. A happenstance, or premeditated? Nursing a glass containing copious amounts of tonic and ice and one small measure of vodka, enough to give her courage but insufficient to make her reckless, she cut a lonely figure. Her legs were crossed tightly enough to reveal just enough firm thigh—just the right amount to suggest a hint of promise above her skirt line, only a smidgen of imagination required. Encased in vertiginous heels, her feet were twisted around the stainless-steel pole of the stool. With one hand she held the stem of her glass and with the other she toyed with strands of her hair while darting sly looks at the group of wrestlers whenever a shout arose from their rabble.

Emilio, satisfied and feeling cool in his musical selection, jumped from one stool and bounded to climb the carefully placed empty one next to the mystery woman.

'Hi there. Can I buy you a drink? What would you like madam?'

His false extraversion was like buds bursting from garish dahlias in a premature spring. Josefina felt a flash of irritation—was this excitable little fellow going to cramp her style, block the channel for seduction of the wrestler she had in her sights this evening? And then Emilio took the roll of notes from his inside pocket and her vantage suddenly looked somewhat more positive.

'Order anything you like, for tonight I am a winner.' He swaggered.

With the crinkling notes serenading her, she flashed him a lipstick-framed smile. 'Oh, thank you sir. I'll take another vodka and tonic please. And congratulations on your success.'

*

The caravan felt eerily quiet without Emilio's presence. Emiliano was accustomed to his brother just being there: when he went out, his brother remained, and when he returned his brother was still there. He was surprised to realise how much he missed the slow turning of the pages of the latest book Emilio would usually have his head buried in, the way he muttered the words just beneath his breath as he read.

His unsettled energy resonated with the lingering vibrations of their earlier contest and the celebratory post-match frenzy of congratulations in the changing rooms. Paying back the borrowed adrenaline, Emiliano was experiencing his body coming back into balance as it always did. Sadly he'd never trained his mind to do likewise—it just kept spinning and swirling, eating up what little energy he had remaining, a restless show pony constantly anticipating the next rodeo.

As he flung the caravan door open to the

uncharacteristic quietness outside, the absence of human sounds provided no distraction from his solitude. Practised in wheedling into the centre of any communal activity, an exaggerated abandonment crept in. In their infancy, Maria, being stretched so thinly between her roles of cleaner, cook, mother, and housekeeper, had by necessity taught her boys to self-soothe. At nighttime, once she had settled them into their shared bed, she would leave them to find their own paths into sleep, while she, in the adjacent room, the connecting door left slightly ajar, would cut vegetables and fry beans for the next morning's breakfast. Emilio had found solace within himself much easier than his brother; Emiliano always fought fiercely against accepting his ultimate aloneness in this world. He would protest so loudly from their small bed, sheets and blankets wrestled aside, to the point of fraying Maria's nerves so much that finally she would succumb, pick him up. Plonking herself in the chair by the window, she would rock him asleep in her weary arms.

This evening, with the absence of his mother to comfort him, he grabbed his jacket and ran off into the night in search of the company of his brother.

Imagine the scene he encountered on entering the bar: an attractive young woman mirroring the body language of his quiet, introverted twin, both perched on bar stools, she exposing her neck and displaying her soft cleavage as she threw her head back in peals of laughter in reaction to something he had just whispered in her ear.

The woman's eyes widened and her jaw fell in an unflattering way as she registered that in this room was not only the Little Man she had been flirting with, but his mirror image. The only visible difference was that one man remained seated on the bar stool smiling softly, while the other stood beside her with greedy eyes feasting on her breasts, displayed precisely at his eye level.

'And who do we have here?' questioned the newcomer, as if he were striking a conversation with her bosom.

'So, there are two of you. Two minis,' she declared, clapping her hands. 'How exciting! What fun!'

Emilio, by this age so bored of the amusement the presence of both twins provoked, merely raised his eyes to the heavens beyond the bar ceiling. 'We're not objects of fun. We're two adults, with adult thoughts, adult emotions, adult needs and wants.'

Josefina jolted as if a small electric shock ran through her—her evening's mission was in danger of slipping beyond reach, just as she had been making good progress. These guys, she could tell, needed empathy and flattery, not mockery. Reconnecting with her years of experience in seduction, she focused on the prize.

'So, tell me…' she began, adjusting the shoulders of her dress, knowing it would pull her neckline lower. '…were you also a victor in the ring tonight? Are you also a man of valour and victory?'

'But of course!' Emiliano lifted his gaze to meet hers. 'I can achieve anything my brother can. We are a team.'

*

When Lillibet walked into the bar she was somewhere between damp and soaking. Rain droplets settled on her bowler hat, luminescent like tiny pearls. The blackness of her hair, enhanced by the rain, glistened under the neon lights. The hem of her skirt, having trailed through puddles in the unmade pavements, was rimmed with a murky carelessness. The whole bar turned to look at her, not because she created much sound beyond the rush of air as she opened the door, but because her presence brought an ominousness.

A vague unsettled feeling had compelled Lillibet to be among her kin this evening, that maybe her unease could be abated by companionship. The moment she had stepped over the threshold a chill running up her spine told her she was mistaken.

For one so attuned to reading the intentions of others by micro changes in their faces and body movements, she was curiously bad at diving below the surface displays that transpired in social settings. So, when she saw not just one but both twins flirting with the unknown woman at the bar she misread two things: firstly, that this woman was shallow of spirit and fragile of ego, in need of adoration to assure her place in the world. Secondly, that the twins had each easily moved on from her in their affections, which logically meant the previous emotions they had expressed were fickle and as weightless as a feather caught in a summer breeze. Had she more experience of love, had she even indulged herself in romantic novels, she would have been aware the common way most of us disguise our hurt is to cover the wound. To cover it so thickly we can no longer poke a finger into it and displace the energy as it slowly settles, forgetting that although the scar tissue may knit together, it will forever be fragile.

Abruptly turning her back on the display of outlandish sexual chemistry, Lillibet walked studiously erect, suppressing the message her heart was giving to her body to collapse into limpness. She greeted her compatriots with a brave smile.

'Which one of you ne'er do wells will buy me a drink then?'

*

In advance of that evening, Josefina had already decided it would be her last hurrah. She had made, or more accurately *stolen*, enough money to subsidise her legitimate teacher's earnings, cover her rent and retain her independence for at least the next three years. Financial forecasts from the economists were predicting a change in fortunes by then: the downward plunge would stop and maybe reverse. She had read enough novels to know a person's greed for more than their fair share, way beyond what was needed, would lead to hubris. And that never ended well.

Her self-promise couldn't have anticipated that the evening's prey would comprise not one but two victims. Two Little People, eager as adolescents to be led astray. Two small men, each with a tightly rolled stash of bank notes in their trouser pockets. Two men who had something to prove to the world, each other, and, if she was reading the signals correctly, to the curious woman in the bowler hat and muddy hemmed skirt.

Would she be tempting the gods if her final seduction was of two men? Did the robbery of two simultaneously count as one or two crimes? And if so, would it be recklessly greedy to pursue this path? But they were inseparable in a manner that lay somewhere between frivolity and interesting. Somewhere between love and hate. Somewhere between economic freedom and imprisonment.

Casting a glance around the bar, she took in the looks shot in her direction by other luchadores, contributing to her growing unease. Her upbringing hadn't trained her in the thought processes of a criminal mind—she was on rocky territory. Had she been spotted in one of these bars with the wrestlers one time too many? Was someone about to realise the correlation between her presence and the subsequent chain of robberies? Luck was possibly slipping through her fingers like sand through an egg timer. Sooner or later the vessel would be empty. It was time for action—one last time.

'Hey guys, why don't we get out of here? I know somewhere much more comfortable where we can relax, and you know, get to know each other a whole lot better.' Josefina smoothed her skirt over her hips, imitating a caress.

Emilio, still revelling in his newfound acceptance of adventure, jumped from his stool, landing firmly on both feet.

'Sure! What are we waiting for?'

Stealing a look at Lillibet to check if she was bearing witness to this other woman making moves on him, he registered that her focus was elsewhere, amid the crowd. There was no way of knowing what her tender heart was doing. He had to make himself care less. He had to drown his feelings for her before they drowned him.

Emiliano, never one to usually accept the role of bystander, was nevertheless experiencing a desire to retreat. Something just didn't feel right: Emilio's behaviour had an undercurrent of recklessness which he wasn't resisting, coupled with an aura of deviousness permeating the air around this woman. With a curvy figure combined with a lovely face, she could have captured the attentions of any man in the bar, so why was she so focused on his brother? His new sense of fraternity wasn't willing to leave anything to chance—he wasn't going to allow his guileless brother to head off into the night alone with this woman. Wherever they were going, he was going too. Plus, he might just get in on some action!

'Oh, hold onto my arms or I may topple over in these heels,' the woman giggled as they exited the bar, one twin on each side. She towered above them like a gaudy steel and glass office block obstructing the sun.

'Where are we going?' asked Emiliano, as he noted the unfamiliar street names in this unfamiliar town.

'Don't you worry about anything buddy.' She giggled. 'I know the perfect place for us. I'm going to treat you in a very special way you'll never forget.' She tapped her painted fingernails on the hard casing of her clutch bag as if it contained the secret to all pleasure.

'And what do you expect in return?" he asked bluntly.

'Just the satisfaction of giving you guys some sweet, sweet pleasure.'

Emilio skipped along the street. A slightly drunken innocent.

*

The hotel was no place for someone of olfactory sensibilities. It reeked of mould trapped in the back of neglected cupboards. It smelt of despair.

The presence of the concierge was tokenistic: the door

keys he slid over the high counter to guests were tied to a heavy brass keyring discouraging theft. He never met the eyes of the guests; his role was merely to accommodate, not to pass judgement. Josefina longed to explain to him 'This is not what it seems' each time she returned to the hotel with fresh, intoxicated prey. But to do so would have necessitated explaining not only what it wasn't, but what it was. Her need for safety was ten times greater than her need for the approval of an unknown paternal figure.

The composure of the concierge slipped this evening as Josefina entered the seedy foyer propped up on either side by the twins. A hint of confused recognition passed his face as if their faces were familiar yet unplaceable. Something protective within him wanted to suggest to the twins that ascending the stairs with this woman was unwise. His inner voice challenged the place from which this feeling emanated—why shouldn't they enjoy some sensuous pleasure? Who was he to judge? Yet something wasn't right.

After handing Josefina the key he turned up the volume on his small radio, his solo companion which could always be relied upon to both distract his thoughts and drown any undesirable noise from the bedrooms. The twins and Josefina scrambled up the stairs accompanied by the tympanic refrain of a late nineteenth century orchestral piece.

Josefina calmly unlocked the bedroom door and ushered the twins into the darkened room. Each piece of furniture was silhouetted, lit only by the waning moon shining through the smeary window. Emilio stumbled over a crease in the worn carpet.

'Be careful there,' she whispered. 'Don't hurt yourself.'

She wanted this to be over as quickly and uneventfully as possible. She wanted to leave this claustrophobic room and never touch the pink nylon bedspread, never hear the rattle of the ill-fitting wardrobe doors, or smell the stale regurgitated air . She wanted the last of her ill-gotten money in her pocket, these small guys safely knocked into a temporary sleep and to rid her life of Sebastian and his toxic bravado. She wanted to reset her moral compass and never again shift from her true north.

'One last hurrah,' she muttered to herself. 'Make yourself at home boys,' she chirped, picking up the carefully pre-placed box of matches with which she lit the few candles she had previously dotted around the room in a paltry attempt to create a romantic atmosphere.

'Who are you really? What's your real name?' asked a voice out of the shadows. She spun around sensing one twin studying her silhouette as she sidled around the narrow pathways between the furniture and walls. Maybe the fresh air and the walk had begun to sober him up? If so, this was bad news.

Carefully placing her clutch bag on the window ledge behind the dust laden curtain, she swiped a trail of ants marching in line with the concentration of a tiny army. Emilio had removed his shoes and was lying back on the bed singing quietly under his breath, while his brother sat on the edge, his shoulder girdle held rigid and firm. It was obvious to Josefina that Emiliano was on the precipice of slipping beyond the threads of the web she had so carefully woven.

Sitting next to him on the bed, she placed her right hand on his left knee and moved just close enough for him to inhale her perfume, to smell the womanliness of her. The candlelight allowed her to see his features in outline only, so she had to utilise her other senses. As she slid her hand up his thigh, she listened acutely. And in this listening, heard his breath quicken. The silken web strands were once again being pulled tightly. She leaned forward and kissed the side of his neck: it tasted of sweet sweat. It tasted of anticipation.

Emilio, sensing he was being excluded, and determined to no longer be the spectator of his brother's life, slid his buttocks across the shiny eiderdown, moved Josefina's hair aside and began to nuzzle into the crease where her neck met her shoulder. She jumped, slightly and then giggled in a girlish way. Both twins echoed her laughter back until the room swirled in joviality.

'We need a drink, just to relax us all a little more. How about a drink, boys?' She stood, stretched, and yawned like a languorous cat, reaching her elegantly manicured hand out to seize the bottle she had previously tucked beside a few magazines on the scratched formica coffee table.

'Ooh, what is that? What have you saved for us?' Emilio asked gleefully as he rolled back on the bed, kicking his feet in the air.

'Vodka,' she replied. 'Let me pour you each a good, strong drink to celebrate our meeting. It's going to be such a fun night ahead, isn't it?'

'Let me help you,' offered Emiliano, climbing from the bed.

'No, no, you are my guests. I invited you here. It would be my honour to serve such virile champions. You both lie back and relax.'

Suspicion was still dancing on the edge of Emiliano's

consciousness. Nevertheless, he was drawn with a force of desire to enjoy the pleasure of this woman. It would be respite from the jangle of his restless mind trying to make sense of how and why things had fallen apart with Lillibet. Climbing on the bed he lay side by side with Emilio. Locking his fingers behind his head, he reclined as if on a sun-kissed beach and enjoyed the vision of Josefina moving around the room. She was a magician, pulling glasses out of thin air, creating sensuous shadows on the wall.

'Boys, I'm short a glass. I only have two. Allow me to offer you each a drink first, then I'll take my turn.'

Their upbringing, the manners Maria had drilled into her sons, still ran deep.

'No, no,' they cried out in unison. 'We can't possibly drink before you. You must have the first drink.'

Josefina was unsure if one twin or both had professed this. It didn't matter. She felt hot, hot and a little clammy. Something in her belly was burning. Her plan wasn't exactly falling into place this evening, but it was going nowhere near as smoothly as her previous seductions. She had to concentrate; having gotten them this far into her lair, both as excitable as puppies, she mustn't now let them slip away. *Think of those crisp banknotes. Just this last time*, she muttered to herself like a mantra.

'Why don't you two share a glass, and I'll have the other?' she suggested.

The twins looked each at the other and then, in synchronicity, shifted their gaze towards the wall. 'We don't share stuff,' said Emiliano bluntly. 'We may look alike. We may have once shared our mother's womb. We might have shared childhood clothes. We might share a passion for the same sport. But that is where the sharing stops.'

Josefina wasn't going to challenge such a strident stance, even if it was beyond her comprehension. His consistent staccato tone left no space for negotiation. There was to be no sharing. *Count to three, keep breathing*, she told herself. *Then try again.*

'Boys, you are my guests. I have invited you here. Let's not get hung up on old fashioned courtesies around drinks. You will each have a drink from your own glass, then I will follow, and then we can get down to having some real fun. Okay?'

She winked twice, once for each twin. Heaven forbid they be expected to share one wink!

'But first I need to freshen a little, if you know what I mean.' The twins both nodded at her. They didn't know in detail but felt obliged to go along with the aura of feminine mystique.

Picking up her clutch bag, Josefina headed to the bathroom. Behind the closed door she carefully placed Sebastian's meticulously prepared phials on the window ledge. As her hands trembled, she registered gratitude for Sebastian's habit of always providing her a spare phial, 'in case of spillage', he would explain in a somewhat condescending tone as if she were a toddler prone to tipping up her cup of juice.

She loathed his patronising manner as she recalled how he would look her straight in the eye and repeat: 'Remember, use one bottle only. The contents are so precisely calculated—just enough to knock a grown man into a deep, deep sleep, but not enough to kill him. Perfect!'

Now, she had two men, impatiently anticipating her return to the bedroom. Thank goodness for the extra bottle tonight—one bottle for each twin.

After pouring generous measures of vodka into each glass, she carefully emptied the phials, one into each drink, and remembered to put the empties firmly back into her bag. Leave no trace.

Reemerging from the bathroom, she consciously gave her hips an exaggerated swing, carrying a promise. 'Nearly there,' she thought. 'Nearly there.'

'Cheers boys,' she giggled as she passed a glass to each with an encouraging nod. They in turn obliged, knocking the drink back with one bold swig each. Emiliano returned the glass to her with expectation bordering on entitlement. Emilio passed his glass back with an expression of gratitude.

Josefina meticulously rinsed out one glass in the bathroom sink, poured herself a good measure of vodka, and climbed on the bed between the twins. Wrapping a well-toned arm around each small shoulder, she drew Emiliano into the right side of her neck and Emilio into the shadow left.

'Let's just rest and relax a little. Enjoy this moment. We have all night.'

Emilio and Emiliano's eyes met across the undulation of Josefina's breasts. They shared an unusual, yet precious smile. And then each gently closed their heavy eyelids, releasing themselves from short lifetimes of resistance.

Epilogue

It was only later, when the nervous policeman knocked on Maria's door to break the tragic news, that the villagers heard her scream soar down the whole mountain valley in a torrent of pain without possible solace.

It was only later, when Miguel had boarded the bus, that he realised as soon as he arrived home he would forever hold his children closer than close.

It was only later, when Pilar found herself kneeling before the church altar, that she realised truly how little control humans have of their fates. And the power of prayer to provide comfort.

It was only later, when Josefina had thrown the rolls of banknotes into the river and washed her hands, that she acknowledged to herself she would never escape the weight of her conscience. Never.

It was only later, when Lillibet visited Emilio and Emiliano's small, serene corpses laid side by side in the lily-scented funeral parlour, as she stroked their cold cheeks, that she whispered to each of them just how much she loved them. And always would.